After Dinner Conversation Themes
Philosophy of Religion Edition

Philosophy | Ethics Short Story Fiction

After Dinner Conversation *Themes* – Philosophy of Religion

This magazine publishes fictional stories that explore ethical and philosophical questions in an informal manner. The purpose of these stories is to generate thoughtful discussion in an open and easily accessible manner.

ISBN# 979-8-9924170-7-4 (Print)
ISBN# 979-8-9924170-8-1 (Digital)

Library of Congress Control Number: 2025945791

Copyright © 2025 After Dinner Conversation®
Editor in Chief: *Kolby Granville*
Edition Editor: *Derek Kocher*
Story Editor: *R.K.H. Ndong*
Copy Editor: *Kate Bocassi*
Cover Design: *After Dinner Conversation*
Design, layout, and discussion questions by After Dinner Conversation.

https://www.afterdinnerconversation.com

After Dinner Conversation is an award-winning independent nonprofit publisher. We believe in fostering meaningful discussions among friends, family, and students to enhance humanity through truth-seeking, reflection, and respectful debate. To achieve this, we publish philosophical and ethical short story fiction accompanied by discussion questions.

Table Of Contents

FROM THE EDITION EDITOR .... - 4 -

THE ANGEL IN THE JUNIPER .... - 5 -

GRIEF .... - 16 -

PNEUMADECTOMY .... - 31 -

THE HOUSE OF GOD .... - 42 -

THE SACRIFICE .... - 49 -

GOD IS ALIVE .... - 63 -

SACRIFICING MERCY .... - 79 -

IN THEIR IMAGE .... - 94 -

THE DEVIL YOU KNOW .... - 117 -

TWO LEFT ARMS .... - 127 -

AUTHOR INFORMATION.. - 143 -

ADDITIONAL TITLES .... - 146 -

ADDITIONAL INFORMATION .... - 147 -

* * *

From the Edition Editor

When I first came across *After Dinner Conversation* I was intrigued by the idea. After reading a few stories I knew this was exactly what I was looking for to help create more engaging conversations in my classes that all students could more easily participate in.

Having now tried out a few articles at various levels I have seen engagement improve and gotten feedback that the students have enjoyed reading the stories. As I have embarked on updating and reshaping my philosophy courses I felt: What better time to try to put together a set of creative short stories to supplement academic readings?

As I began planning a Philosophy of Religions unit I came across some stories in *After Dinner Conversation* that I knew could be very useful and engaging for class. It has been an enjoyable challenge to put together this collection of ten stories that relate to various aspects of the Philosophy of Religion.

These stories range from topics dealing with the characteristics of God, the authority of God, the issue of souls, the problem of evil, religious experience, religious belief, and the concepts of faith, as well as miracles, how we should live, the concept of heaven or the afterlife, and of course dealing with the devil.

As we know there is not a more contentious topic to discuss than religion, but I believe these stories can create a safe springboard to begin launching deeper conversations about the topic. I hope you enjoy reading these stories as much as I did and that they create a desire to discuss the underlying themes/ethical issues they cover. There are many more engaging stories I wish I could include but I will leave you a list below of a few of them so that you can delve into the archive on your own.

- "Have a Nice Eternity" - Nov '21
- "Idle Horns" - Sept '20/Sept '22
- "Simon" - Feb '21/Aug '23
- "And God Said" - Apr '22
- "The Price of Moving On" - Aug '24
- "Heroes" - Nov '23
- "Father Dale's Drive Thru" - Feb '21
- "Exodus" - Nov '21
- "Momentary Paradise" - Feb '23

Derek Kocher – Edition Editor

The Angel In The Juniper

Sarah Johnson

* * *

Content Disclosure: None

* * *

Old Clyde Adamson was plotting with the Jacobin faction.

Holly, who had studied under him only the subjects he taught on the side—Neoplatonism in the early Church Fathers, and Classical Drama—had been hired on a month ago as his secretary, and was now perfectly sure.

It was disturbing. One couldn't deny that the present republic had degraded to the mere form of representative government under the last president and his hand-picked parliament, but the Jacobins were dangerous—low-profile activists who had formally concluded that the governmental system no longer admitted renewal by legitimate means, and were prepared to incite even revolution to restore the principles of the four-hundred-year-old Constitution.

Holly didn't know yet how deeply Prof. Adamson was involved with the faction, or how high a member he might be. She felt sure that, with his broad scholarly reputation and influence, he could hardly fail to be a decisive force in the group. But the thought that the boss she so liked and respected could be a treasonist hardly alarmed her more than the inevitable, gastric knowledge that this brilliant man knew, or would very soon know, that she knew. And would address the fact, to protect himself and his party. Somehow.

That gastric knowledge turned to a squadron of armed butterflies when Prof. Adamson came in that morning and said quietly, "Miss Granger, I wonder if I can ask you to join me on a stroll into Warbell Wood this afternoon? I feel it's time I introduced you to someone there, someone closely involved in my work. Please don't be alarmed, Miss Granger. This can mean nothing personally harmful to yourself, unless you voluntarily choose to undergo certain risks in support of a noble cause. You are under no threat or duress of any kind—only the invitation to learn about something you may consider important."

While looking at his face—ever-same, good-humored yet earnest—she could not fear or distrust, and agreed; but when he had gone to his lecture hall, could do both with a vengeance. She told Mrs. Parsley, the bursar, where she was going that afternoon, and left a note instructing her to contact the police if Holly wasn't back by 10 p.m. (No use if the police had found something more profitable to do, like arresting a dissenter, but supposing they hadn't.)

Afternoon came, and so did Adamson.

"Take your coat, Miss Granger. And have you any heavier shoes? The going will be rough."

It was.

Holly was surprised to find how well Adamson seemed to know his way, where there was no path, and how vigorously the old man could forge through the thick brush and bracken of this less-frequented part of Warbell Wood, a sylvan enclave that edged bustling Old Fruit Market Square, but, bottlenecked between two suburbs, eventually widened and stretched for miles into the hills. Holly thought herself athletic, but was frequently left several paces behind, gingerly poking at a spray of barbed hawthorn or caught by the stocking to a tough bramble.

It was easier here, amid a dense growth of dusty ferns; Holly kept easily by Adamson's side, and could even join in conversation. She had caught scraps of commentary through the branches, and knew he was trying to explain something about morality and the appeal to divine authority, but could only begin to pay attention now, in mid-lecture.

"I'm saying this because very soon, in about fifteen minutes, you'll meet a man who lives out here nearly all the time. Before I tell you what he does, I need to know your own conscientious view of the work of the Jacobin faction, with which you must be a little familiar. How do you..."

His voice trailed off through the foliage of a juniper while Holly was forced to stop and get a twig out of her shoe. She raised her head to call, "Please wait a moment, sir—"

And didn't call.

Holly had never seen an angel, but knew that was one sitting in the juniper tree. Flowing haired and broad jawed, hardly female, hardly male, picked out in a dazzling clarity that made the surrounding greenery seem blurred, it reclined on the branch with the easy balance of a seagull, a figure which seemed spatially paradoxic—compared to the branch, a miniature person, yet full of an aplomb that gave the impression of giantism.

"Holly."

She teetered a step nearer, still holding one shoe.

"Adamson is a traitor of the worst kind, Holly. He has turned against his own nation and the government that provided for his career, and is even now coordinating an armed rebellion, to break out in a few days. He is leading you to a meeting with an even more dangerous conspirator."

"Wh... what can I do?" lisped Holly.

"You must prevent the rebellion. Adamson's disappearance will paralyze the Jacobin communication network. You must kill him."

Holly staggered to the juniper's trunk and leaned, panting.

"Out here, before you get any closer to the radio shack where his accomplice works. Where no one will hear a sound. Since he joined the rebels, he always carries a sharp, double-bladed hunting knife in the breast pocket of his coat. Very soon it will fall accidentally on the ground. Watch for it, snatch it without his seeing, then carry it secretly until you see a chance to thrust it under his ribs. Hide his body in the bushes, then walk downhill until you find running water, which will lead you out of this wood. In two weeks, the search for him will expose some of his incriminating papers, which will prove beyond the slightest doubt that he was on the verge of inciting revolt. It is then you must announce your deed and reveal his body. You will save the peace, and all the lives that might be lost by warfare.

You will receive the praise and thanks of your nation, and with good reason."

Holly pressed her closed eyes to the bark.

"Go, Holly. Great matters depend upon you. The time is short. God will speed and nerve you. Go, daughter!"

Hardly knowing what she was doing, Holly stumbled hastily through the branches, now following the voice she realized was Prof. Adamson's, and which was calling her name again and again. "I'm coming, sir!"

"You're tired," exclaimed Adamson anxiously when she appeared through the boughs. "I've hurried you too much. I'm sorry, Miss Granger. I was anxious that we would not be followed. I felt you could be trusted. I know your strong conscience, and your concern for good administration, in the college and in my office, and I feel sure you must hate the abuses of the present legislation. Do you read the leaflets by 'Socius,' the anonymous Jacobin writer?"

"I have, sir," murmured Holly. A disturbing memory. The little pink leaflets, occasionally appearing overnight on doorsteps or park benches and eagerly collected by public-minded citizens before the police could confiscate them, contained very little political commentary, but only excerpts from the secret minutes of the current Parliament, which revealed how deeply rotted with bribery and nepotism the lawmaking body had become. The State's frantic efforts, not to disprove, but suppress their content, was only too solid evidence of their accuracy.

Something glinted on the ground. As soon as Adamson turned to thrust forward among the beech saplings, Holly unthinkingly caught up the fallen knife and clutched it, under her coat against her pounding heart.

"What do you think of Socius?" asked Adamson, over his shoulder. "What do you think of his contentions?"

Holly was too honest not to admit, "I have—I have found them very penetrating, sir. Very well attested."

"And you agree," grunted Adamson, holding back a branch to allow her to pass, "that our system of suffrage and referendum has been narrowed almost to preclude the chance of reorganizing parliament or the presidency by legal means?"

This touched a sore place in Holly; her own voting privilege had been revoked for life, like so many others', when she let her Public Pedestrians' license lapse for just two months. "I... have to admit, it seems that way."

"Do you love our nation, Miss Granger?" Adamson had stopped, to look in her face. "Do you want to see our ancient constitutional rights restored?"

Oh, how wonderful that would be. No more night raids. No more drafts for ruinous foreign wars without popular consent. No more arbitrary, commerce-withering tolls and taxes... Old, forbidden subjects taught again in the college...

Oh, mercy. The angel, the knife.

Holly trembled all over before she could catch herself. Adamson took her arm. "My dear, are you well? I've exhausted you! Sit down, over here, on this root."

How he reminded her of her courtly old great-uncle Everard; how she wanted to confide her battle to the man she had just yesterday regarded as a pillar of dependability and wisdom. How could the angel call him a "traitor of the worst kind?" How much about him she must not know! If not for the angel, she would be utterly convinced by now that he was an ardent patriot, and a humanitarian driven only to the possibility of violent revolt by a far more violent tyranny. But, if God were on the side of the present regime...

"Sir, will you repeat what you were trying to tell me earlier, about moral decisions and divine authority? I think I'm ready to listen."

"Gladly, Miss Granger. I was telling you about Socrates's 'Euthyphro dilemma.' Basically, it states that moral laws are often said to rest on God's authority, as in the Bible. Yet it's conceivable that God could order someone to do something obviously immoral, as in the case of Abraham ordered to sacrifice Isaac, or even schizophrenics who believe a voice in the head telling them to commit crimes. This dilemma is often used in academia to discredit a religious approach to moral problems.

"The trouble is, in the absence of divine authority, all moral law becomes a social, even at a more basic level *neurological*, construct. There's no appeal to abstract ethics, only to more common or historically affirmed patterns of behavior, sometimes the appeal to species survival, which always beggars the simple question—'Why?' ...So I remain a theistic moral agent. You see, I got around Euthyphro long ago."

"How, sir?" murmured Holly, half unconsciously fingering a shape under her coat.

"Don't you see? The dilemma assumes that something or someone, making a claim to be the Creating Mind good enough to overcome all reasonable doubt in the hearer, demands an act which breaks the universally recognized moral laws every faith and culture attributes, or has attributed, to the Deity—the laws that forbid murder, and, and perjury, rape, infanticide, thievery and vandalism, acts a culture's code must always go to extraordinary lengths to justify under any circumstances!—Miss Granger, not all *violence* is immoral. In very unusual circumstances, passivity is immoral. I want you to think about that as we climb this hill. But the test of a so-called divine voice is rather simple—nothing demanding a plainly immoral act can be the God who made the rules! God cannot change His mind by definition. All that's changeable is temporary, while that from which the temporary, changing world sprang, must be eternal and changeless. Moreover, all evil itself is a secondary product, the perversion of an original good. The creator, however, cannot be secondary, but primary—therefore wholly good."

"Then what if," Holly was vexed and embarrassed to hear her own voice whine pleadingly, "what if something that made every other claim—something outside and independent of this physical world, something... like you say, *primary*, independent of space and matter, suggested—an act—that *seemed*, only *seemed*, a little off, and you couldn't be sure—what was really right—wouldn't you be safer to obey?"

"Wipe your face, you're perspiring," said Adamson, passing her a folded cotton handkerchief. "I hurried you too much. I knew it."

Holly buried her damp face in the cloth, then emerged as suddenly. "Sir, my question?"

"Is that even a question, Miss Granger? You aren't safer to obey an immaterial being. If we premise that God laid out moral laws, then you're safer to obey Him, or *them*, for they're the same thing."

Holly felt herself at last on sturdy grounds of objection. "Sir, I can't agree. You mentioned two necessary qualities of

God—goodness, but also that independence of the changing, temporary world. If a being is independent like that, it must follow from your own statements that that being is good." Her dizziness now was a different kind, not terror but exaltation. She saw herself convincing the old academic that her heavenly messenger was legitimate. She saw herself avoiding murder by persuading him to fulfill the angel's command himself, by abandoning or betraying the Jacobins.

Adamson reached and pulled toward himself a delicate huckleberry sprig, faintly smiling.

"Are you nearly ready to go on, ma'am? It's not far now. Perhaps you've gathered by now why we're climbing this great hill to reach our destination."

Holly wasn't thinking about hills.

"Nearly ready, sir. A couple more minutes. Just tell me. If an obviously immaterial, independent, primary sort of being told you that—that, for instance, the Jacobin side was really in the wrong about our country's future, that leaving the current regime in place and—and trying to peaceably reform it were better, would you reconsider?"

"Do you think I'd reconsider if *you*, sitting on that root, told me positively that the Jacobins were mistaken and the regime were reformable? With no more supporting evidence? Just that? Seriously!"

Holly wanted for a second to hide her face again, then thrust her jaw out.

"But *I'm* not an angel!"

"What difference? Haven't you ever heard that the Devil is a perverted angel? Not all that's immaterial is God. Part of *you* is immaterial, but *you're* not God!"

She was not in a frame of mind to play exhaustion long, and jumped up. "Well, if it's not far, let's go."

"Wait, Miss Granger. I mustn't, I can't, reveal my contact out here or his work before I know where you stand regarding the work of the Jacobin society. If you're against the prospect of violent revolt, I'll walk you back to town before it gets any later."

"I'm in favor," she blurted, turning a straining face toward another juniper tree; "I'm in favor," she repeated more loudly, swinging her perspiring forehead toward him. "Let's go. I'm not tired at all." But when he rose, she made an urgent gesture and took his arm.

Adamson walked easily on the rising ground, lightly supporting her arm on his rigid elbow and sending earnest, good-humored glances over the hazel brush and young beeches, carrying his native land toward civil war with every stride, yet serene in the confidence of his own moral system, grounded upon a God he had never seen, in which he placed such confidence precisely *because* of the not seeing.

And at his side scrambled Holly, keeping very near his ribs and trying to make her hand bring the knife from her coat and shove it under them, ever more feverishly convinced of the morality of the act, grounded upon a God she had seen, in which she placed such confidence precisely *because* of the seeing.

* * *

This story first appeared in the After Dinner Conversation—April 2021 issue.

Discussion Questions

1. Professor Adamson references "Euthyphro's dilemma," where Socrates asks Euthyphro, "Is the pious loved by the gods because it is pious, or is it pious because it is loved by the gods?" What does this phrase mean, and how does it relate to Holly's problem?

2. Like Abraham being asked to kill his own son, do we have an obligation to obey God, even when it goes against our moral code?

3. Professor Adamson argues that God's morality is, definitionally, unchanging and timeless. Do you agree that morality (*from God or otherwise*) is unchanging and timeless? How does Holly's answer to the question affect her choice?

4. The story cites the mass removal of voting rights, night raids, rising taxes, and the near impossibility of legally changing the government. What, if anything, would be the "last straw" that would cause you to take up arms to violently overthrow the government?

5. Professor Adamson argues that "not all *violence* is immoral. In very unusual circumstances, passivity is immoral." Do you agree? Can you think of an example where passivity is immoral?

* * *

G r i e f

Steven Ross

* * *

<u>**Content Disclosure**</u>: None

* * *

Part 1 – Denial

Guided by turbulent winds, a piece of trash tumbled under trees and lit street lamps. It rolled against brick buildings, sometimes getting caught on furnished outcroppings. It traveled toward me and stopped by my feet. The wind threatened to blow it away, so I leaned down to pick it up. Someone had torn a piece of newspaper and crunched it into a misshapen ball.

I dreaded the discovery, but I unfolded it anyway. The headline of the shredded paper confirmed my suspicion. My stomach churned as I read the words: "God left us." I wept at the reminder and sat down on the curb. As the tears started to dry, I realized I loosened my grasp on the paper. It blew in an unknown direction for another poor soul to read.

Except for the individuals lost from civilization, the world knew of His departure. On a normal day like any other, the holy beacon shone in the sky for all to view. The signal announced a forthcoming decree. As tradition, the news avenues of every nation publicized the holy pronouncement.

As a bishop of the faith, I arrived at the palace amphitheater to experience His will and presence firsthand. The atmosphere vibrated with enthusiasm and excitement from the gathering crowd on the sacred grounds. We didn't have to wait long before the palace doors opened. God came out to the balcony that overlooked us and said, "It's time for me to leave. I have taught you everything I can. Goodbye."

He retreated into the palace, and the doors slid shut. Moments later, loud rumbling emanated in front of the crowd and tremors could be felt under us. The holy palace broke free from the ground and levitated into the heavens. Everyone sat in silent disbelief.

He existed as a central part of our past. Since the dawn of our people, he has guided us on the path of righteousness. From his palace, he appeared throughout history to teach us spirituality and technology. I didn't believe this could be the end. I searched for a reason as to why he would leave. Nothing came to mind.

I stood up from the curb and wiped the wetness from my face. The stormy wind had subsided but now, night nestled in the city. My duty dictated that I comfort my congregation. They waited for my interpretation of the events. The appointed hour of meeting passed as I roamed the streets to hide from my obligations. There would be those that stayed behind at the house of God. I decided to defy my inner doubt, so I started in the direction of my temple.

My sermon would be pointless without God's influence. I tried to find inspiration as I ventured through the sparse streets. Few roamed the avenues; those I saw glanced at me with sullen, pleading eyes. They recognized my holy garments and wished for answers. I resolved to listen to them on the way to my destination.

I journeyed in silence till an elderly woman waved me down. She shuffled closer and pulled her scarf tight to protect against the chill in the air. I asked, "How might I help you, ma'am?"

She said, "Bishop, I see the strain in your eyes even in this light. Have faith and hold onto it." She gave a slight smile and continued her walk.

After, I ventured on the sidewalk when a young couple, holding a small child, stopped me. The mother looked at me, tension visible in her posture, and said, "Bishop, we're afraid. Who will protect us?"

"God. He always has and always will."

The baby started to cry, and the couple apologized. They gave their thanks then moved on. I resumed my path until I nearly collided into a balding man reading a newspaper. He eyed me up and down, and said, "Bishop, I missed the news because of my night shift at the factory. Are the headlines true?"

"Yes. But fear not. His will still guides us."

The man shrugged, looked back at the newspaper, and flipped it through. I began my walk anew and approached the final street to my destination. From a side alley, a haggard, gray-haired man bumped into me. I almost fell, but I kept my balance. The man reeked of sweat and unwashed clothes. He gave me a slight nod. I said, "Don't worry. I'm not injured, friend. Join me at the temple. We have fresh clothes, warm food, and a washroom."

The man seemed taken aback, but managed to say, "I appreciate the offer, Bishop. I'm happy on my own."

"God will guide you on your own journey. If you ever change your mind, the temple is open."

The man performed a polite bow and went on his way. I surprised myself with my responses tonight. I doubted God and myself, but He remained to help me on my way.

I arrived at the temple and opened the doors. My eyes grew wide, and my heart beat a bit faster as I witnessed my full congregation in attendance. A smile formed at the wonderful sight of so many faithful. I let the doors close behind me and I trod on the crimson red carpet to the podium.

When I arrived, I pivoted to face the crowd, and said, "God will return to us."

* * *

Part 2 – Anger

O righteous God,

What have we done to deserve this? There's so much more for you to teach us. We made offerings and we prayed for you. We wanted nothing more than your protective presence. Our people have been led astray by our own hands. The sacred city is now a cesspit of corruption and crime. Don't you see our suffering?

After my prayer, I rose from kneeling at the shrine. My shins ached because of the wear the tuffet endured the previous month. Countless faithful visited the sanctum at my temple, but the steady stream ceased this week. I practiced my faith alone on this occasion. It had been a month since God left but many had forgotten their faith. My entire congregation stopped attending and the laity had diminished to nothing. I witnessed the contempt in their eyes, day after day, because God didn't grace us.

The other bishops of the city fared worse. The faithless performed sacrilege on the resting place of our absent God. The populace ransacked the other temples, looting sacred texts and idols. They brought them to the pit where the holy palace had resided. Previous petitioners turned rioters built a bonfire on the remains of the hallowed items.

My temple survived the turmoil by virtue of my faith. I convinced the city police to provide extra protections surrounding my place of worship. Their resolution faltered with each passing day. I barricaded the temple for the inevitable. Without the steadfast guidance of God, people were frightened.

I snuffed out the candles of the shrine and ventured into the main chamber of the temple. I walked to the entrance vestibule to check the barriers I put in place. The reinforced boards remained intact and covered the windows securely. I headed to the stairs on the opposite side of the enclosure.

The twisting staircase led to the domed second floor. Along the vault, stained glass depicted events from history with God. Below the colored glass, unprotected windows allowed a view of the surrounding streets and buildings. I doubted people could reach them, so I left them untouched. I peered out and witnessed a gathering crowd. A barricade set up by the police blocked them from getting too close. Armed police stood behind the metal fence.

The protestors displayed diverse signs of libels. Some read: "Liar," "God is no more," "God, the coward," and "God will never return." My faith faltered at the hate shown by the once loving people. My belief in God led to the life I lived today. My dream of forever being in God's loving embrace turned into a nightmare.

* * *

O God,

I don't understand your will. You made us whole. Now, we're fractured for eternity. You left us to be like this. You did this. The suffering of the people is your fault. You made your choice. I've made mine.

I didn't bother kneeling as I said my prayer to God. The cushioned stool had been destroyed in the ransacking of the temple. The candles of the shrine were strewn on the slate floor. The sanctum had fallen into disrepair. I grabbed my satchel that I had laid on the ground and glanced about one last time before I left.

The main hall fared worse. The pews, where so many faithful sat during holy liturgy, were broken apart. I viewed the shattered remnants of the podium where I conducted my sermons. Dirty, muddy footsteps stained the deep red carpet. Warm air wafted into the room. The boards I placed in the vestibule failed to protect the temple.

I climbed the staircase to the second floor. When I reached it, my footsteps crunched as I stepped on broken glass. I arrived at an alcove where there used to be a grand mosaic of God. The rioters chiseled away the picturesque tile leaving a mess of brick and grime. Everything had been destroyed by the looters and all imagery defaced. The priceless holy objects were stolen and brought to the bonfire in the pit of the palace.

To the side of the small enclosure and behind rubble, a hidden compartment in the wall remained untouched. I struggled at first, but I moved the debris blocking it. The wall appeared as any other except for the brickwork in the corner. I pressed a brick in the wall, and a click sounded. I placed my hands against the wall and moved it upward. As the section of the wall lifted to a certain point, it latched into place.

A small cache of sacred items stood out amongst the dark of the concealed compartment. The valuables were artifacts collected during my early days as a bishop. I placed my carrying pack next to the hiding spot. I unlatched the leather piece holding it closed. My bishop garments laid inside it. Tears welled as I prepared for the culmination of my life's choices. I emptied the compartment's contents into the bag, secured them, and closed the satchel.

I placed the carryall over my shoulder, headed down the stairs and left the building. I walked out into a hot, muggy day. I looked to the sky and witnessed the rising plume of black smoke. The bonfire on the remains of the holy palace still burned. I tightened my grip on the strap of my bag and ventured toward the once holy ground.

With every step, my decision seemed more justified. He left us. God built his people to fail, the coward. The smoke became denser as I arrived at the bonfire. I could barely breathe, and my eyes stung. I walked down the steps of the amphitheater and stopped within a safe distance of the fire. I lowered my satchel to the ground then opened it. I pulled out a relic, held it in my hand, and threw it into the fire. One by one, I removed a holy item from the bag, and hurled them into the flames. I ran out of sacred pieces, but my bishop garments remained. I closed the satchel shut and chucked it into the bonfire.

* * *

Part 3 – Bargaining

As soon as I shut my eyes for sleep's respite, guilt burned in my chest. If only I had been more faithful, my belief could've shielded against rash decision-making. My uneasy rest caused my waking hours to be a mess. My responsibilities piled up as I tried to manage them all. Today, the archbishop called an emergency meeting to unify the last bishops. Riots and looting continued without end. I gathered my remaining courage and left my apartment.

Rain clouds riddled the sky, and droplets fell as I headed to the main temple of our faith. The grand temple survived the onslaught of hate because of the holy guard. The small order of soldiers protected the temple with their life. The order's lineage could be traced back to the initial discovery of God. They remained steadfast in their duty to protect the first temple.

When I arrived, a member of the holy guard stopped me and asked for my credentials. I presented my ID card and the guard let me pass. Once inside, I traversed the ancient halls. The architecture had been preserved since the first meeting with God centuries ago. As I continued further, I walked by rare relics and paintings lining the walls. They had been kept safe over the history of our people as a testament to God's influence.

The main temple's creation cemented our dedication to God so many years ago. The building resided next to God's holy palace which had been discovered where the pit burned now. Around the holy palace and the grand temple, a metropolis formed over time. It used to be the heart of our civilization until God ripped part of it out. I stopped that line of thought before it led to anger.

I arrived at an empty meeting room. I sat myself at the

table and waited for the others. I checked my watch, and the appointed time had passed. I decided to linger a bit longer. Someone walked into the room. He wore plain clothes and hat, but I recognized the man as a fellow bishop. Others trickled in after some time.

A door opposite the entrance opened, and the archbishop, in full golden regalia, entered. All the bishops stood in unison, but she motioned for us to sit. She removed her crown and placed it on a cushion on the table. She sat on the throne at the head of the table and said, "Thank you for coming during these dire days. I should've called for a meeting sooner."

She sat in silence, while studying each of us. She continued, "Only a few of us remain. I'm at a loss as to what to do. If only we had seen this coming. We could've prepared or convinced God to stay somehow. What if God was upset with us for an unknown reason? These problems plague my thoughts." After she finished speaking, she stood and walked over to the window that overlooked the bonfire.

I struggled to say something meaningful. I couldn't formulate a response. The quietness continued until one of the bishops got up and exited without a word. A few followed his example. I remained with the archbishop and a couple other remaining bishops. If I stayed, maybe God would see our struggle.

The archbishop cleared her throat and said, "So many have lost faith even among God's chosen. My faith is faltering. However, we must keep to our duties. I know most of your temples have been looted. I'm giving you permission to use this temple for worship. If we can unite the people again, order will be restored. I'll leave further instructions with the captain of the guard."

She left the room. I felt empty after that encounter. She echoed my own sentiments. I hoped that her plans would help ease my doubt. I exited the meeting hall with the remainder of the bishops. We didn't say a word to one another. Each had sullen eyes as I imagined mine were the same.

We met the captain of the guard near the exit of the building. He handed us our orders. I headed out and opened the sealed envelope. It gave details on the pockets of the city where looting and protests had been less severe. We were to go to these locations to find the devout and convince them to go to the temple. Once they arrived, we could discuss the ways to bring peace to the city.

Anxiety swelled in my mind, and I felt its weight in my stomach. I doubted my determination to see this through. I couldn't even keep my congregation together. It would be impossible to convince others to rejoin the faith. If only God never left, everything would be normal.

* * *

Part 4 – Depression

"The archbishop has stepped down. The faith's hierarchy will be dissolved. The holy guard will remain to preserve the grand temple and its artifacts."

I laid in bed as I watched one news program after another discuss and debate variations of those sentences. Similar stories played on all the city's news channels throughout the week. The faith lost its leader. My duty as a bishop became obsolete. I wished I hadn't been useless. I tried to gather more followers, but people scorned me at every chance.

Light crept into my apartment, but I pulled the blinds

shut to block the midday sun. I curled up under my blankets and covered my head with a pillow to block the world from sight. My mind raced and I couldn't concentrate on anything. I tried to empty my mind, but self-doubt crept back in. I pulled the pillow to cover my mouth and I screamed into it. The muffled shout sounded pathetic. Frustrated by my futile attempts to clear my mind of perturbed thought, I sat up in bed and glanced about.

My apartment appeared to have grown smaller the past few days. The trash container overflowed. Dirty dishes covered the countertop. Clothes piled up on every surface. I hadn't used the shower or even washed my face in days. I felt my chin and discovered a scraggly patch of hair. It seemed impossible to attempt self-care. My stomach began to rumble but resting in bed until this nightmare ended seemed to be a better idea.

Tossing and turning failed to quell the hunger. I rose from bed, struggling to sit upright. Weariness weighed on me. For the last few days, takeout had been my main source of food. I decided to go to the grocery store located a few blocks away. All my clothes were dirty, so I donned the least unkempt articles.

I opened my apartment's door, crossed the threshold, and walked into the empty hall. Arriving at the stairs, I descended them and exited the apartment building. Sweat formed on my brow within one step toward the grocery store. A heat wave had hit the city. I glanced about the street, and a few people were on my side of the sidewalk. I wanted to avoid all human contact. When someone neared, I glanced at the concrete sidewalk and continued walking. My foul state caused me disgust so I imagined others would feel the same.

I reached the grocery store and entered. The store's air

conditioner blew cool, fresh air onto my warm face. The sensation helped to break the train of negative thought. As I searched for food, people gave me a wide berth. I attempted to avoid their attention, grabbed any food nearby, paid at the front register and left the store.

With my bag of miscellaneous goods, I began the trek to my apartment. The afternoon sun intensified the heat to an unbearable level. With the added weight of my groceries, I struggled to continue so I stopped at a park on the way and discovered an unoccupied bench far from any onlookers. My stomach growled as I sat down. Something in the bag had to help with my hunger. I found a candy bar, took it out, and tore it open. It looked so appetizing, but I put it back in the bag.

Anxiety outweighed hunger. On repeat in my mind, I envisioned the newspaper heading, "God left us," from the day God removed himself from the world. I felt sick so I leaned back on the bench but that made me want to vomit. I placed my bag on the ground and laid on the bench, closing my eyes.

I felt someone shaking my shoulder. I squinted to see a man looking down at me. I rose from the bench and realized I'd fallen asleep for a couple of hours. I rubbed my eyes to clear off the remaining weariness. The fellow gestured down at the bench, and I scooted over to give him space to sit.

I evaded human contact all afternoon and now I sat in silence with a stranger. I glanced at the ground to see my groceries were strewn all around the bench.

I heard the man clear his throat, and he said, "Bishop, do you remember me?"

My heart raced at hearing the word "Bishop." I shifted and studied the man. He appeared to mirror my unkempt persona except he had gray hair. After some searching, I remembered meeting the man outside of my temple the day of God's abandonment. I said, "I do. I offered you respite at my temple, but you refused."

The man nodded and said, "I see you've fallen on hard times. I can tell why. Most have been affected by him. Before and after he left, he influenced this world. My life hasn't changed, why should yours?"

I stared in disbelief, but I couldn't answer. We sat in silence for some time before he got up and said his goodbye. I gathered my scattered groceries and walked home. I made it into my apartment, shut the door, and laid in bed, not bothering to take off my clothes. I curled up and wept.

* * *

Part 5 – Acceptance

I traversed the streets to my old house of worship. Except for the grand temple, the temples' properties would be sold off to help heal the city from the unrest. I arrived at my temple and perceived a construction crew active at the site. I tried to walk past the gated-off area that surrounded the location, but a tall, brown-haired worker stopped me.

I asked, "What will happen to this place?"

She said, "We are clearing it out and repurposing it into an elementary school. Please head out. It's not safe, you could be injured."

I said a farewell and left. Old feelings of regret surfaced but the place would be put to good use, so they subsided. I wanted to visit where the holy palace had been, so I headed there. It had been an overcast day, but slight raindrops fell now. By the time I turned the final corner to my destination, the rain poured. I climbed down the amphitheater steps.

At the remains of the old bonfire pit, the steady rain kept the ashes from blowing away. I missed God and the days of debate with the other bishops that occurred here. I reminisced for a while longer before leaving the once holy grounds. I vowed never to return because of the possibility of old wounds reopening.

I had to look forward to the future. My calling in life ended when the fires of faith diminished. I had been so focused on my own problems that I failed to see the state of the city and the world. People were hurt and scared. My own despair affected those around me.

I should've acted differently. The world couldn't go back to the old ways. We could manage with a new way of life. I exited the steps of the amphitheater and saw the grand temple. I gleaned from a news program that the site would become a museum.

I gathered my courage and headed for the front entrance. Plywood covered most of the windows and side entrances. When I arrived at the main doors, I attempted to open them, but they didn't budge. Someone saw my struggle. An elderly gentleman opened the door, poked his head out and asked, "Want do you want?"

I said over the sound of the rain, "I would like to apply for employment at the museum."

* * *

This story first appeared in the After Dinner Conversation—January 2022 issue.

Discussion Questions

1. In this story, the people believe in God because God lives among them. Is that "faith," or is faith only possible in the absence of proof? Is faith, or some other word, the best word to describe what the people have?

2. In the story God says, "It's time for me to leave. I have taught you everything I can. Goodbye." What do you think God means by this? Does it mean God is incapable of teaching them more, they are incapable of learning more from God, or something else?

3. Is God, definitionally, unable to be a person that lives on earth and instructs and teaches us directly? What is the definitional difference between God and an omnipotent being?

4. If you had absolute proof that God did not exist, would it change your morality, values, or duties to others and why?

5. Why do you think the people of the story so quickly abandon God's teachings once he leaves?

* * *

Pneumadectomy

Harris Coverley

* * *

<u>**Content Disclosure**</u>: Strong Language; Medical Procedures

* * *

Rolly stood for a few minutes in the shade of the large oak, just out of sight of the boys gathered on the dry shaven green of the bowls club. All aged around eleven like himself, they were dividing up their meager numbers for a game of soccer, knowing that since it was a Friday afternoon, the pensioned members of the club would not be bothering them. The light was getting a bit dim, but the warmth of the midday sun was still in the air.

Rolly knew Patrick and Liam well enough—they had been friends going back to reception class—and had seen the other six boys here and there; the tallest with the ginger hair he was sure was called Lachlan. And how long had it been since he had had a good game of footie? Not for a good four months, not since the operation, and certainly now with his recuperation period over and his mother finally letting him go out again, albeit with her hands knotting as she allowed it, it was high time to get a game in, just like he used to.

Deciding it was safe enough, Rolly ventured out of the shadows and onto the green.

As soon as they saw him, the boys stopped their pregame selection chat and turned to look at Rolly in silence.

"Hi guys," Rolly said meekly, with a weak and perhaps overly pathetic wave of the hand. "How's it going?"

The silence continued for a moment, until Liam broke it: "Not so bad Rolly, we're just about to play soccer."

Rolly and the group stared at each other for a while in renewed silence, before Rolly got up the courage to ask, "Erm, can I join in?"

The group looked at each other.

"I'm sorry Rolly," Patrick ventured, struggling with his words, avoiding eye contact. "We can't really let you... our parents said so... it's just... what with you... not having a soul anymore an' that."

Rolly felt a lump in his throat. His breathing cut short and he had to consciously suck in air.

"But..." Rolly started, "but..."

"Just fuck off no soul!" Lachlan suddenly shouted, stepping forward, arms out, both hands in fists.

Rolly suppressed a whimper and advanced, trying to maybe get Patrick to talk one-on-one, away from the group.

Lachlan lost his nerve with the others, and they all counteracted with a step backwards. His aggression was just a front; he was just as terrified as the others.

Rolly surveyed the cowed faces of his former friends and acquaintances, and without another word turned away from them and began a brisk walk home, wiping his tears on his fleece sleeves along the way.

* * *

The discovery of the soul came about by complete accident. It was Pram Bhatia of the University College of Medical Sciences in New Delhi who made it when investigating an anomaly in a teenaged patient who had been admitted to the Guru Teg Bahadur Hospital with severe cramps in his lower abdominal region. A scan showed what at first appeared to be the usual suspect of appendicitis, and Bhatia as assistant chief gastroenterologist was preparing a quick removal. That was, until he noticed something odd about the scan, something he had not seen before. Risking his professional credentials, Bhatia chose to wait out the patient's pain and see what happened. His bloodwork had not shown any sign of infection. The poor young man lay in agony for a day, two days, three days... and then suddenly, nothing. No pain, no discomfort.

Bhatia performed another scan and saw the anomaly had reduced, but was still present. Being a graduate of engineering with a background in medical scanning—which had gotten him interested in gastroenterology in the first place—he went over to the university's engineering school and with the help of a few students modified an old CT scanner to a completely new frequency. He used the cobbled-together monstrosity to scan the patient anew, and saw what no human being had seen before. Within the appendix of the young man was something *different*, not material, but not wholly immaterial either. It was a presence, a force of some kind, attached to the body but through some unknown bond.

He scanned other patients with his device and managed

to find variations of the anomaly in each one he examined. He even instructed his assistant to scan himself, and found the anomaly within his own appendix.

When the original patient was being discharged, Bhatia caught up with him and asked him how was doing. He said he would be feeling confident... if not for his sweetheart leaving him just before he was admitted. Bhatia asked him when this had happened, and he replied a day before the pains began. Bhatia asked him if it had emotionally hurt him in a great way, and he replied that yes it had. Bhatia asked him if he had questioned his belief in god after her departure, and the patient—a self-proclaimed devout Muslim—reluctantly admitted that, yes, he had.

Bhatia set to work on a paper straightaway, describing the patient's symptoms, the scanning frequency he had used, and data on repeat observations. At the end he put forth a hypothesis: he had not only discovered the human soul and its place in the body, he had discovered that its welfare could be influenced by our beliefs, our actions, and our emotional states.

Published in the *Indian Journal of Pathology & Microbiology*, the paper was quickly passed around the globe, Bhatia treated as a laughingstock by medical students and surgeons West to East—until Professor Samantha Strong of MIT Medical reconfigured her own scanner and replicated Bhatia's results. Soon, the results were being replicated through testing and examination in medical schools in Berkeley, Chicago, Bonn, Lyon, London, East Anglia, Moscow, Kyoto, Johannesburg, Buenos Aires... the sum of evidence gathered suggested that only Bhatia's hypothesis could be accurate: there was such a thing as the soul, and it "lived" in the appendix.

What had long been thought to be cases of IBS, intestinal infections, psychosomatic referral, and a whole host of other abdominal ailments could now be explained by an appeal to a higher force—although it was later shown that such cases were fifty-fifty on whether they were truly soul related or actually gastronomic in nature.

A whole new school of medical science, post-mystical psychopathology, had been discovered, and with a new international research program, it was to help patients the world over, if not save the lives—or souls—of thousands, millions even.

The world, with the exception of a few stuffy metaphysical materialists, felt good—there were souls, and in all likelihood there was a god or gods, and an afterlife of some sort where the soul would go to meet them.

However, Bhatia, becoming an international superstar appearing on all manner of talk shows and with a book deal from a major international publisher, was the first to point out a very unfortunate problem: What about those who had had appendectomies?

Repeat examination of dozens of excised appendixes by the scan showed there was nothing to be seen by way of a soul—it was just the remains of a lump of prehistoric intestine, not the temple of *Dasein* that it had quickly become in the collective mind of humanity. New scans showed that the soul had not migrated to elsewhere in the abdominal cavity, or anywhere else in the body. And yet those with appendectomies carried on as normal, as though the soul had no impact on the person. They laughed, they cried, they aged, they died—just like those with appendixes.

However, the conclusion was still undeniable: Those without appendixes *did not* have souls.

* * *

Rolly was lying in his bed, thumbing through a Roald Dahl book from a box set his aunt had gifted him while he was recuperating. He really wanted to read it properly, but the rejection of yesterday still weighed heavily on his mind, and instead he closed it and put it on his bedside table.

He lay for a while, pondering certain questions of mortality that would otherwise not have bothered him until the sour beginnings of puberty, until his mother, a short, dowdy woman in a brown pantsuit with long, flaky yellow hair came into his room to kiss him good night.

"We'll go to the city center tomorrow," she said as she pulled the cover up over his arms. "We haven't been there since you came out of the hospital. I'll take you to the big bookshop, and then we'll have something nice to eat, how about that then?"

Rolly just looked dead ahead to his wall with the generic robot and fast car posters, still lost in existential thought.

"Well?" she asked him, squeezing his right arm gently.

"Sure," he replied quietly, and began to slink down under the sheets, his eyes still wide open.

"What's the matter?" she asked him, sitting on the side of the bed and rubbing his right hand.

Rolly turned his head on the pillow to her and said, "I don't have a soul."

His mother almost groaned: *Not this again, please not this again...*

"Well, you know Rolly," she said, taking his hand in both of hers, "like I've said before, the science of it all isn't exact, and it's only been a few years since all this soul stuff started... give it another few years and it'll turn out it was in the right little finger all along, probably."

She smiled as she twiddled his right little finger. Rolly remained stoic.

She stopped twiddling and they were still for a moment.

"Why did you decide to take it out?" he suddenly asked, looking away from her.

She swallowed and tried her best: "Well, Rolly, you do know, I mean, you were in agony, *fire* you said to me, *Mummy stop the fire hurting...* you were on the kitchen floor..."

Rolly was still.

His mother stood up and kissed him on the forehead: "Rolly, if my baby is in pain, something has to be done about it. It wasn't ideal, nothing about an appendectomy is ever ideal, even way back when, but it was the only way... don't let it get you down, or let others get you down because of it. They're all idiots and bullies anyway..."

The boy remained silent. Feeling defeated, she walked to his doorway and switched off the light. Just as she closed the door she mumbled something about eggs Benedict for breakfast and it clunked shut.

As Rolly still stared up in the darkness, it was now his mother's turn to shed tears.

* * *

A week later, Rolly walked alone to Mrs. Jeffries's front door and knocked, the hard wood hurting his little bony fingers as he tried to rap on the veneer like he had seen in films.

The woman had been completely alone in her house since her husband had left her, at least that's what Rolly's mother had said to him. She lived down the street in a large brown brick semidetached house, and Rolly had noticed that at night when he had passed it in his mother's car there was always a single solitary light on in the front room, no shadows moving. He waited nearly a minute before Mrs. Jeffries answered in what looked like a black maternity dress, despite definitely not being pregnant.

"Oh," she said, seeming surprised even though it had been prearranged, "Rolly, you're here, your mother rang, please come in."

Rolly thanked her as he walked into the front room, and saw that the light he had observed previously had been coming from the single exposed bulb of a floor lamp sat next to a red, torn armchair, the seat grayed and almost bare.

He refused a drink and sat down on the opposing couch, while Mrs. Jeffries took to the chair.

She asked him how school was going, relayed that she knew he was a bookworm and asked him what he was reading, and told him how much he was going to enjoy secondary school in a couple of years' time, but all Rolly could concentrate on was the picture of her son Cioran above the mantelpiece. It had been taken at a wedding when he was about eight years old. He was giving a big smile in an ensemble of a dark blue waistcoat and red bowtie, and for some reason was holding onto a pool cue.

Rolly had known Cioran, and had liked him quite a lot.

Eventually Mrs. Jeffries stopped her questions, fatigued from a lack of sunlight, and took a long sip from a cup of cold tea.

When she put the cup back down on the table, Rolly finally asked her what he had been dying to ask since he had come in: "Why did Cioran have to die?"

She had known the question was coming, in some form or another, but it still startled her. Young boys could be very direct when they wanted to be.

She took another sip of tea and said, "I didn't want him to, oh god, I didn't, but it was the only way."

"But... he's not here anymore," Rolly replied with true innocence.

Mrs. Jeffries stood up and walked over to the mantelpiece. She stroked across the portrait picture with one hand, and rolled the burnt wick of a short yellow candle with the fingers of the other.

"Do you believe in heaven Rolly?" she asked him, not taking her eyes off her dead son's image.

"I don't know Mrs. Jeffries," Rolly replied cautiously. He genuinely did not. The life of a boy his age was supposed to be dominated by questions of toy blocks and chocolate bars, not ones of theology and thanatology.

"Well, that's where I think Cioran is," she said, not turning away. "That's where he's waiting. If there's a god, it was all part of the plan... his appendix inflaming, the antibiotics not taking hold... all god's vision."

Rolly allowed her some time with the portrait, before declaring: "I don't have a soul anymore."

"I know Rolly, I know," she said, finally turning to face him. "That was your mother's decision, and I respect it. I hope she respects mine as well."

Rolly suppressed another whimper, and looked down into his hands.

The motherly instinct returned to Mrs. Jeffries's mind,

coming over to give Rolly a rub on the shoulder, forcing a pale smile, and giving to him the very last of the biscuit bars from the cupboard that had, many months ago, been Cioran's domain.

Rolly crunched down on the treat as she ushered him out, telling him not to worry, to remember that his mother still loved him, and that she would not mind if his mother popped in for a cup of tea whenever she felt like it.

He thanked her for her kindness and for a while after, as he walked back home, Rolly did feel a great deal better for having talked to Mrs. Jeffries.

Mrs. Jeffries shut her front door as she waved Rolly off, and returned to her increasingly destitute armchair. It was not her time for crying; she had done enough of that already. She resumed her acquired pastime of staring at the wall, waiting for Death's forgiving hand, the coolness of the coming evening draining in from the outside.

* * *

This story first appeared in the After Dinner Conversation—January 2022 issue.

Discussion Questions

1. Do you believe a person has a soul? If so, where do you think it is kept? Where does it go when you die? What purpose does it serve?

2. Assuming the story is true, and people do have a soul, would you be friends with someone who had had their soul removed?

3. What seems to be the practical effect (*if any*) on the person of having their soul removed? Would you change anything about the way you live your life if there was absolute evidence of a soul?

4. Would you be willing to sign a piece of paper, and sign it with your bloody thumbprint, that said, "The holder of this paper has purchased and owns my soul," and sell that paper to someone else? If you don't believe in a soul (*question one*), shouldn't the paper be meaningless to you?

5. Who do you think made the better choice in the story, the parent who had their child's soul removed to save them, or the parent who didn't have the soul removed and let them die? Given the facts of the story as true, which decision would you have made if you were the parent? (*or for yourself?*)

* * *

The House of God

Shannon Frost Greenstein

* * *

Content Disclosure: Mild Language

* * *

"I don't want to go," the child declared defiantly, and his mother felt her headache ratchet up another notch.

"I know you don't. And I understand why. But we still have to go, so *please* find your other shoe and put them both on."

She was almost entirely successful in masking the strain in her voice, a talent she had developed by necessity over the last several months as she navigated single motherhood with her son and his newly diagnosed autoimmune condition. But now, there were only twenty more minutes before Mass was scheduled to begin, and they were *still* not in the car, and she was starting to lose her grasp on the threads of her rapidly fraying patience.

"But *why* do we have to?" whined the boy, bottom lip thrust forward, grubby fingers clutching a single shoe. "Why can't we just stay home?"

The woman, fully occupied with brushing cat hair from the child's dress shirt, sighed deeply and paused in her grooming. She wracked her brain for the reason with which her son would be least likely to argue. Unconsciously, her hand rose to hover over the crown of his head; then it dropped suddenly like a weight to fall by her side.

"Because the Bible says blessed are those who dwell in the house of God," she finally responded. "And going to church is how we honor Him."

The woman clutched her fingers into fists as she fought the urge to run her hands through the child's thinning hair. She had always loved how his golden curls felt like silk; it was taking a gargantuan effort to break the habit of caressing his head. She tried not to notice the new bald patch directly behind his ear. Curly blond strands littered the boy's pillowcase every morning. His hairbrush next to the sink now held more hair than his head. The dermatologist said it would eventually become clear if they were dealing with alopecia areata or alopecia totalis, and— unfortunately—the passage of time seemed to be suggesting the latter.

"People are gonna stare," the boy muttered after a long silence, tracing the pattern on the bedspread with one finger, refusing to meet his mother's eyes. He brought his own hands to hover near his head, his own fingers clutched into fists, before yanking them back down to his lap as if they were misbehaving.

The pain behind her breastbone took the woman's breath away, and for a moment, she was unable to speak. Her heart ached for her son, and her brain raged at the world, and she was struck with a wave of such impotence that even her steadfast faith in Jesus Christ began to tremble.

"Of course they won't!" she began, one of the many rote recitations of motherhood designed more for the comfort of one's young than to impart any truth whatsoever. Then she stopped, because the truth was she *couldn't* comfort her young—not about this, and not anymore. People *were* going to stare, they had *already* been staring, and there was not a single thing she could say to take this pain away from her child.

Instead, the woman knelt down until she was on the same level as her son and tipped up his chin with her forefinger.

"You are delightful. Losing your hair does not change that, and I feel *bad* for the people who stare, because they aren't *half* as delightful as you."

The boy allowed her to fold him into a hug, even though his own arms remained motionless by his sides.

"Remember... you are special because God made you. He loves you exactly as you are."

She released the child and discreetly wiped away the tears that had formed in her eyes, then handed him the baseball cap, which had been his constant traveling companion since the alopecia diagnosis.

"And you will *always* belong in the house of God. Now, *please* find your other shoe."

* * *

"The peace of the Lord be with you always."

"And also with you."

The woman clasped the hand of the congregant to her left and murmured a demure, *"Peace be with you."* Then she turned to her right and nudged her son, still seated upon the pew, feet dangling well above the floor.

He stood obediently, avoiding eye contact with the

parishioners around him, then dropped to his knees when the time came, behavioral conditioning at its finest.

"Take. Eat. This is my body which is given to you. Do this in remembrance of me."

"Amen."

The boy's mother rose and edged out of the pew, joining the line of congregants assembling for Communion like obedient ducklings. She tugged the boy behind her by the hand, the fingers of his other hand fiddling self-consciously with the patchy hair at his temples.

They meekly approached the altar, the routine eternal and stalwart, ingrained like breathing. Madonna and child, they bowed their heads before the priest, partaking together in the miracle of transubstantiation. The woman prayed to be made worthy of Christ's love; the boy prayed for his hair to grow back.

"Little boys who wear hats in church go to Hell."

The speaker was elderly and stooped; the hat perched on her head like an anachronism was garish, its angle haughty, its veil formal and stiff. She spoke from over his shoulder like a conscience. For a moment, her voice was indistinguishable from the voice he heard in his head when he prayed very hard, something the priest called the *still, quiet voice of God,* and the boy was still dazed when he opened his eyes to glimpse the old woman's sneering face.

"Little boys who wear hats in church go to Hell," she repeated, then opened her mouth for the sacrament like a baby starling. The stained-glass windows threw their light upon the altar as she chewed, illuminating her face in a rainbow of color, the entire scene seeming to the child like a fever dream from which he could not awake. Struggling to her feet, making the sign of the cross, the old woman treated the child's baseball cap to a final scathing glance, then turned and hobbled back to her pew.

Then it was just the boy and the sanctuary and the silence. And the boy was alone.

* * *

The child was quiet as they drove.

"Are you okay, darling?" his mother questioned more than once, and he would nod, and heavy quiet would descend again.

"That woman just didn't understand," she attempted again, glancing worriedly at her son in the backseat. "She's just old-fashioned. I bet she doesn't even know what alopecia *is*. You didn't do a single thing wrong."

Finally, as they were turning into the driveway, the boy spoke.

"Momma, if God is choosing to make my hair fall out, then why did Jesus say *God is love*?"

His mother blinked.

"And if He can't make it grow back, why did Jesus say *with God, all things are possible*?"

The car had come to a stop, but the woman sat immobile, staring into the rearview mirror. Recognizing the beat-up Toyota and its motley crew of occupants were dangling over a metaphorical precipice, she rummaged for something to say, searching for an answer she already vaguely understood she would never find.

"Well..." she began, then paused. "He... God *is* love, honey. Your hair... well, it's a disease..."

"Then why won't He stop it?" the child interrupted. "How can He be God if He can't fix it?"

"He *can*," she reassured her son, immediately falling back

on a lifetime of faith in the omnipotence of her God. "He just…"

But while faith is a comfort, it's not much of a compendium, and the woman found herself foundering weakly through this declaration. Still waiting for the right words to arrive in a flash of insight, her voice eventually trailed off into nothingness.

"I prayed for Him to take away my alopecia," said the boy mildly, "and He didn't. Either He doesn't want to, or He can't."

The child unbuckled his seat belt and opened the door, exiting the car without further comment, while his mother watched his departure with a slack jaw. Taking a minute to gather herself, shaking her head briskly like a dog, the woman finally gathered up her pocketbook and hurried after her son into their modest house.

She found the boy sprawled on the couch, gazing vacantly at a brightly animated Sunday morning cartoon. His dress shoes had been kicked off; his hands were once again curled into fists, held in his lap through sheer force of will.

"Are you okay, angel?" the woman inquired nervously— though why she should be nervous around her own *son* was still not entirely clear.

After a beat, he glanced up to meet her eyes, staring straight through her skull and then into her soul. The woman took a quick step backward, heat rising through her sternum like magma.

"I don't think I want to go to church next week," the boy remarked. Then, returning his eyes to the television, he casually swept the cap from his head.

* * *

This story first appeared in the After Dinner Conversation—April 2023 issue.

Discussion Questions

1. If you were the mother in this story, how would you answer the boy's questions about God allowing his sickness and hair loss?

2. Epicurus argued as part of his "problem of evil" that God cannot be (1) all-powerful, (2) all-knowing, and (3) all-good because evil (*like children's diseases*) exists in the world, and therefore, there is no God. This is, essentially, the argument the boy is making. Assuming you believed in God, what convincing counterarguments (*if any*) could you make?

3. Should the mother in the story make her son go to church regardless of his wishes? If so, what reasons might she have for wanting her son to go to church?

4. Should the mother in the story have said something to the person who told her son, "Little boys who wear hats in church go to Hell?" What would you have done (*or said*) in that situation?

5. What are valid and invalid reasons for a parent to force their child to do something they don't want to do?

* * *

The Sacrifice

Kelly Piner

* * *

<u>**Content Disclosure**</u>: Mild Violence; Moderate Intensity

* * *

Lenore balanced a box of donuts on her left arm and her Bible on her right as she rushed up the stairs of Saint Mary's Church as she had done every Sunday for the past year. The top floor smelled of dust and varnish, and black-and-white photos of the church throughout the ages lined the gray walls of the hallway. With no family of her own, she'd formed a new church family, special bonds that she hadn't known since she'd lost her father over ten years ago.

She'd be eternally grateful to her elderly neighbor, Miss Rosie. Lenore had driven her terminally ill neighbor to weekly mass the year before she had died. So impressed by the fellowship and rituals, Lenore decided to convert. She wanted her life to have more meaning than going to work every day at Continental Buffet and paying bills. She dared not say it out loud but had always felt that she had a higher purpose.

Inside the church library, a handful of parishioners quietly spoke and sipped coffee. Cardboard cutouts of the Pope and Sister Teresa stood in the corner near an overpacked bookshelf.

Lenore smiled and laid down the donuts she'd purchased for the group and made her way to the corner table where she joined her favorite nun and a young man, Caleb. Sister Ruth always asked Lenore about her week and often gave her special religious books. Caleb, a minister's son, impressed Lenore with his knowledge of the Bible and his articulate way of expressing his thoughts.

It was only then Lenore noticed that white lilies, the funeral flower, filled the room. She felt a thud against her chest. Had someone died?

"Are you excited?" Sister Ruth asked in accented English.

Lenore pressed her hand against the small of her throat. "It's all I could think about all week. The Big Surprise! Any hints?"

"No, I'm also in the dark. I do know it is a great honor for our parish. The greatest honor."

Lenore's imagination took hold. Maybe funding to finally open the new high school? Or maybe a grant to remodel the nuns' antiquated living quarters?

Her thoughts were interrupted when Ethel, a large, imposing woman, cleared her throat and strode to the lectern. Known as no-nonsense, Ethel delivered only the facts and had never once been described as warm-fuzzy.

"It has been my honor to serve as your confirmation director for this past year. Welcome to your last class. It's been a long journey, but well worth it. You'll each be confirmed at the

Easter vigil next Saturday evening. More details will follow. Questions?"

When no one responded, Ethel clicked on the overhead screen that displayed a large picture of Jesus hanging from the cross. "I know you're eager to get started. A reading from John: 3:16–17. *For God so loved the world that he gave his only begotten Son so that whoever believes in him shall not perish but have everlasting life.*"

She paused. "Let this sink in; *For God so loved the world that he gave his only begotten Son.* How powerful is that? What would you be willing to give up for God? Think about that for a few minutes and then we'll share your responses." She walked to a corner table and made herself a cup of coffee.

A curious murmur passed through the room, and class members glanced from one to another.

Lenore tapped at her temple. Intimidated by the biblical knowledge of her classmates, she'd need to come up with an extra special answer.

Five minutes later, Ethel returned to the lectern. "Let's go, one by one. Miss Lula," she said to the eldest member of the graduating class, a widow who wore colorful scarves and baked oatmeal cookies for special church events.

The old woman nervously giggled. "I'd give up many of my possessions and donate the money to charity. I'd live a modest life and dedicate more time to volunteer work." Her voice trailed off.

"Good answer," Ethel said. "Next."

A young mother clutching a baby spoke softly. "What a great question. I'd like to think I'm already doing a good job, but I could do more. Less TV and more Bible time, more church time."

"Good. Next."

The Anderson family, grandfather, son, and grandson, all took turns giving thoughtful answers.

Lenore thought of feasible responses, but all the good answers were already taken. She flinched when Ethel called on Caleb who sat next to her.

In a forceful, confident voice, Caleb said, "I'm preparing to dedicate my career to God. I enter law school this fall and will specialize in representing people of all faiths who have suffered discrimination and have had their religious freedoms violated."

"Wow," Lenore muttered under her breath. She'd barely graduated high school. Caleb always found just the right words.

A wave of approval filled the room.

"Excellent. Lenore, we saved the best for last."

Lenore's face burned hot. Her mind went blank, but before she knew it, she blurted out, "I'd give up my life for God."

Dead silence filled the room. She hadn't known where the response came from.

Sister Ruth reached over and squeezed her arm. "Perfect answer."

Lenore's insides quivered. She hadn't prepared to give this answer. God did indeed work in mysterious ways.

Ethel smiled. "So glad to hear you say that. Please remember that Jesus was a human being who was tortured and had nails pounded into his flesh and bones. This is no small matter."

Lenore's body suddenly ached, thinking of Jesus's suffering.

Ethel clicked off the monitor. "I won't keep you in

suspense any longer. I know that everyone is wondering about the great honor that's been bestowed upon our parish. Let's move downstairs for the announcement. Please leave your phones in the room as we don't want to be disturbed. I'll lock up."

Lenore and Sister Ruth shuffled behind the others, down the steps and to the chapel. But Ethel bypassed the chapel and led the class down a back staircase.

Lenore hadn't known that the church had a basement. At the bottom of the steps, desks and chairs were stacked in one corner and the room smelled of mold and moisture. Pictures of various saints hung along a long hallway that seemed to have no end.

Ethel faced the group. "What I'm about to say will come as a shock. Our parish has been selected for a great honor. Just to think that our tiny town and parish out of the entire nation...

"Bishop?"

Bishop Hernandez stepped out of the darkness.

Lenore knew it had to be a big deal if the bishop had graced them with his presence. But why meet in a dank basement when they could have met in the relaxing chapel upstairs?

Bishop Hernandez bore a serious expression. "By now, I'm sure your minds are racing with multiple possibilities. Due to the confidential matter, we've met down here so as not to be disturbed." He raised his arms in the air. "*For God so loved the world that he gave his only begotten Son.* How many of you have really thought about what this truly means? For most, it's just words, a Scripture, but today you'll be put to the test."

The blood pounded through Lenore's veins.

"Today, one of you will have the opportunity to repay God. You will make the ultimate sacrifice. Think of all the squalor and immorality in the world. Help heal God's broken heart." Lenore searched the faces of her classmates for what they may be thinking, but all stared intensely at the bishop. She thought of the old reality TV show where someone would jump out and say, "Smile! You're on *Candid Camera*." This was obviously a test, the last hurdle before confirmation. Maybe a church initiation similar to fraternities?

Caleb raised his hand. "What's the ultimate sacrifice?"

Thank God for Caleb. He always spoke his mind.

The bishop stepped closer. "Ethel asked you earlier what you would be willing to give up for God. I believe one of you said she would give up her life?" All eyes landed on Lenore.

"Dear God," Lenore mumbled under her breath. Now she knew this was a test. And just what would they make her do for this initiation? Hold her head underwater until she nearly passed out or force her to read Scriptures for twenty-four hours straight?

She was jarred back to the room by the bishop's booming voice. "God has promised this parish a great gift in exchange for one of the members of our confirmation class to sacrifice his or her life. In return, a member of this parish will be selected to perform miracles unlike any seen since Jesus walked the earth. Think of all the good that can come, not only to this community but perhaps the entire world. The blind will see and the deaf will hear. Even hopeless addicts will receive the gift of eternal sobriety. All this in exchange for one life, one single sacrifice." He stared at Lenore.

Lenore collapsed onto a metal chair. "I don't know what

to say. I did offer to give up my life for God, but not like this."

"What did you mean then?" the bishop asked. "It is a mortal sin to tell a lie in church."

She stammered. "I wasn't lying. I meant it, but I'm not ready to die, not today."

"My dear, is anyone ever ready to die?" He smiled. "But to think that you will inherit the Kingdom of God."

Classmates nervously chattered amongst themselves. Were they all in it together, a carefully orchestrated skit where she'd been singled out just to prove her faith? "This can't be real. It just can't be."

Lenore could feel the steely stares of her classmates. "Sister Ruth," she cried out.

The elderly nun rushed to her side and spoke softly. "God will protect you. Do not fear." As if on cue, Sister Ruth led the class in reciting the Lord's Prayer.

No way would the sister lie to her or be involved in a cruel hoax. Lenore looked to Ethel and then the bishop. She weighed her options. She could ask to be excused. But if she were allowed to leave, she knew she'd never be welcomed back into the parish, the only Catholic Church within forty miles. Plus, if what the bishop said was true, how could she live with herself knowing she'd turned her back on God, her special opportunity to save lives? When she found her voice, she asked, "What if I say no?"

A furrow formed between the bishop's brows. "There could be Hell to pay. Someone must volunteer before the day ends. You've been given the power to change the world for the greater good."

"But why me?"

"Would you like to nominate one of your classmates?"

Bishop Hernandez asked.

Lenore's voice cracked when she spoke. "No, I don't want to do that."

Caleb stepped forward. "Just how did God reveal this special request?"

The bishop signed the cross. "Jesus appeared to two separate parishioners on the same night and made God's request known. It has been thoroughly researched by the diocese and found to be highly credible."

Lenore thought of the old Scripture, *An eye for an eye. A tooth for a tooth.* Maybe God was avenging some ancient sin by claiming a human sacrifice? If so, this was Old Testament stuff. Ethel's voice jolted Lenore back to reality.

"Since Lenore is reneging on her earlier promise, do we have another volunteer?"

Lenore looked into the faces of her friends, but not a single one spoke up. If she didn't play along, she could be Hell bound. If she agreed, who knew what could happen?

"Let's go one by one," Ethel suggested. "Miss Lula?"

The elderly woman held her hand over her mouth before she spoke. "I don't know what to say other than I'm raising my only granddaughter. She's nine, and I'm all she's got."

"Good enough," Ethel said before she moved on to the young mother.

The woman held tightly onto her infant. "I just had a baby. I can't volunteer." Her voice rose. "I can't do it! I won't do it!"

And so it went from the Anderson family, offering perfectly legitimate reasons why they could not be the official sacrifice and leave the earth.

When it was Caleb's turn, he convincingly spoke. "My life has just begun. I've committed my career to doing God's work."

"Lenore?" Ethel said.

By now, Lenore's entire body trembled, and despite being forty, she spoke in a childlike voice. "What can I say? I'm not ready to leave this world. I've left so many things undone."

"You don't have children," the young mother shouted.

"That's right. You once confided in me that you had no one at all." A hint of bitterness had crept into Miss Lula's voice.

The remaining class members took turns confronting Lenore as if her life meant nothing at all.

Finally, Caleb took his turn. "I'm sorry to say this, but you have the least to offer of all of us. You're a cashier at a buffet restaurant. It's not like you're helping people, like a nurse or even a teacher."

She couldn't believe her ears. Caleb was her friend. She'd even attended his father's funeral a few months ago. Her body went numb. "I'd like to leave. I'm not playing this game anymore." Her voice was barely audible.

"I'm sorry, Lenore," the bishop said, "but you couldn't leave if we wanted you to. No one is allowed to leave until the ceremony is complete. You're looking at this all wrong. It's not a loss. Think of it as a great honor, the greatest of your lifetime. A quote from the Book of John 15:13: *No one has greater love than this, to lay down one's life for one's friends.*"

Even Grandpa Anderson shot her a dirty look. "Yeah, you've said many a time that you had no one but yourself. I'm the head of my household."

Lenore thought of her gray tabby, Mercy, at home waiting for her. She backed away from the crowd. "Enough is enough. You're scaring me."

Bishop Hernandez placed his hand on her head. "Accept your fate, my child. God has willed it. You are his chosen one."

"You're good at talking the talk. Now walk the walk," Caleb barked at her.

Lenore placed her hands over her face. Just how far would they go? If this were a test, she was surely failing it. "But God wouldn't want this," she told the hostile group. "He wouldn't want one of us terrorized and threatened. He wouldn't!"

Ethel's eyes opened wide. "Have you not heard a word we've said? *For God so loved the world that he gave his only begotten Son.* And you think you're better than Jesus?"

Lenore shook her head. "I never said that. You're twisting up everything I say. I just want to go home. Please. I'll find another church."

"We'll take a vote," Ethel proposed. "All in favor of nominating Lenore as the sacrifice, raise your hands."

All six classmates' arms shot up into the air.

"The decision is unanimous. Lenore it is."

"No!" Lenore shouted and bolted past the group. At the top of the stairs, she banged on the door. "Let me out! Please somebody help me." Without her phone, she couldn't call anyone to save her.

Ethel moved to the bottom of the steps. "It's no use. Take some deep breaths and pray. You're making this too hard on yourself."

As if in a trance, Lenore shuffled downstairs. With nowhere to run, she'd go along with the church's little scheme. What choice did she have? Still, she hadn't given up hope that at any moment, the group would break out in laughter and pat her on the back. Hopefully, by the end of the day, she'd return to her cozy apartment and curl up with her cat.

The bishop held the Bible high into the air. "In the name of the Father, the Son, and the Holy Spirit, please guide Sister Lenore in making this ultimate sacrifice. Deliver her from evil and present her with everlasting life."

Lenore silently prayed for God to deliver her from this mob scene. Surely God was more powerful than the bishop.

Paralyzed from disbelief, Lenore's vision became fuzzy. Had she fallen prey to a religious cult or a group of fanatics like the Charles Manson family? And not a single soul would miss her until she didn't show up for work on Monday.

Bishop Hernandez left the room and then out of nowhere, stepped out of the darkness, lugging a huge wooden cross behind him. The group gasped.

"Come, Sister Lenore. You will lug this cross as Jesus did on that fateful day. Gather around, class, and offer her words of encouragement."

Accepting her fate to go along with the cruel game, Lenore's legs barely supported her as she inched toward the bishop. This was obviously a reenactment of Jesus's last hours.

"Take this, Sister, as your cross to bear. You will carry it to the end of the sacred hallway."

Feeling as if she were marching to the gas chamber, she leaned the cross against her right shoulder. My God! It must have weighed a hundred pounds. She struggled to take her first step.

"Move!" Ethel shouted.

As Lenore put one foot in front of the other and dragged the cross behind her, it made scratching noises, worse than nails on a blackboard. Beads of perspiration now drenched her forehead, and her white cotton blouse clung to her torso.

Twisted faces of her once friends shouted insults at her as the Romans must have shouted at Jesus. "False Prophet! Blasphemy!"

After a couple minutes, she began panting. "I can't go any farther. It's too heavy."

"Try harder," Caleb ordered her. "You think Jesus complained?"

"Don't let us down," Lula said.

"Do this for my baby's sake and all the babies in the world," the mother pleaded.

Lenore collapsed under the weight of the cross, and it smashed to the concrete floor. "Have mercy on me. Water. Please."

Sister Ruth held a cup to Lenore's lips. Lenore wondered just how far the tunnel extended. For as far as she could see, only darkness.

Sister Ruth helped Lenore to her feet and stood next to her, sharing the weight of the cross with both hands as she walked behind her. "Don't worry. I'll help you," she said, just as Simon of Cyrene had helped Jesus carry the cross on the march to Calvary.

Lenore tried shutting down her weakening mind. She'd just walk. By now, her shoulder throbbed and blisters covered the palms of her hands. Hadn't she sacrificed enough?

And when she thought she could endure no more, a faint light burned at the end of the hallway. Salvation! Just a few minutes more, and she would have passed the test.

A candle lit a stone altar adorned by a photo of Mary standing with Jesus. "Please, Mother Mary, deliver me," Lenore begged.

At the end of the hallway, she and Sister Ruth both collapsed into a pile. Lenore struggled to breathe as she stared up at cobwebs on the ceiling. She silently prayed, *Have mercy on me.*

Ethel and the bishop helped Sister Ruth to her feet and offered her water.

Afterward, the group encircled Lenore while the bishop raised a crucifix high into the air. "Sister Lenore, please place your body onto the cross for the final part of the ceremony." Nearly delirious from exhaustion and thirst, she crawled onto it.

The bishop and Caleb carefully secured her body with strong rope that burned and cut into her flesh. Now, she couldn't move her limbs at all. How much more could she suffer in the name of God before they'd release her? If ever there was a true test of faith...

The bishop and Caleb raised the cross upright and secured it with wire to a post. Lenore looked down at the crowd who stood quietly nearby.

Blood seeped from fresh blisters and ran down Lenore's arm. "How much longer?" she barely managed.

"We're almost there," the bishop said.

"Thank God!" she muttered.

And then, the bishop lifted a hammer and pressed the first nail into her flesh.

In her final moment of consciousness, Lenore raised her eyes to the ceiling and implored, "Father, forgive them for they know not what they do."

* * *

This story first appeared in the After Dinner Conversation—December 2024 issue.

Discussion Questions

1. Assuming, for the sake of argument, this group is actually part of the Christian church, is God's will always to be followed? Is God's will, spoken through the church, always to be followed?

2. Sometimes, people of faith will argue, "God wouldn't ask me to do that," or, "If God told me to do that, I would know it wasn't God." How do you reconcile unquestioning faith in God's will with an individual's ability to decide what is and is not a Godlike directive?

3. Why do you think none of the other relatively new members of the church spoke up in Lenore's defense? Does their reasoning (*fear vs faith*) matter in their own culpability?

4. The other members all have reasons/excuses why they can't be the one who is sacrificed. What (*if anything*) does that tell you about their faith? Should a truly faithful person be eager to give their life for God, regardless of their other social obligations?

5. Why do you think "God told me to do something bad... oh no, am I actually in a cult?" stories are relatively common in western culture?

* * *

God is Alive

Ville V. Kokko

* * *

Content Disclosure: Mild Language
* * *

It was the strangest conversation I've ever had. I still don't know what to think of it. Yet, I cannot forget it.

At that time, I was getting a little worried about my friend, Thomas Cale. We used to run into each other now and then in our small town, and sometimes we would agree to go out for a drink and talk. But for a month or two now, I had barely caught a glimpse of him.

I suspected the change had happened after that visit of his to the city. I didn't know what it had been about, and though I knew he had come back, I wasn't even sure how long he had stayed there. I was lucky to have been aware he was going in the first place. I had run into him by chance when he was going to the train station. He had almost barged into me in his hurry, even though it was a good fifteen minutes before the next train would leave.

I can vividly remember the way he looked then. There was a strange expression in his eyes, opened unusually wide in a kind of awe. Probably there was fear, wonder, delight, and doubt there at the same time. Or maybe this is just hindsight. In any case, I could see that he was affected. By what, that I couldn't get out of him. When I asked where he was going, he seemed on the verge of telling me all about it, but in the end, he said he'd not say anything yet, other than that he had something in his bag that he needed to have examined by experts. It all sounded very odd, but I walked away with the impression he had found some old and valuable antique.

It might have been weeks later when he got back—still too preoccupied to contact me, not even to keep his promise to tell me all about it. I gradually became aware of his presence, but he didn't return to his old habits of being seen around town. Local gossips suggested he was getting holed up in his home and becoming an alcoholic. He still seemed to go to work, at least, but not to do much else.

Now, Thomas wasn't my best friend, and I don't think he had one himself, at least not in our town. I missed him a little and was slightly puzzled as to what was going on with him, but I didn't think of the matter too much at first. However, as time went past, I got worried enough to call him and ask if we could meet, and to insist a little after the initial automatic rejection I'd come to expect. I said outright that I was worried and wanted to know how he was and if he had some problem. After some hesitation, he laughed drily and said he might as well tell someone, and I might be the best one to hear it.

I said I'd be glad to listen, even in spite of his curious warning. For he warned me that if he told me, I might end up like him... though, he added after a pause, probably not. I didn't understand what he meant, so I just said I was willing to take the risk.

It was a chilly autumn evening as I walked out to Thomas's house. The sun shone without warming much, and occasional gusts of biting wind fought over the first few fallen leaves, throwing them first this way, then that. Thomas lived in the older part of town, so my feet took me over slightly uneven square cobbles and down a winding street between houses that occasionally leaned forward as if they were trying to touch their counterparts on the opposite side.

Thomas's house stood some way apart from the rest. Aside from that, it was quite unremarkable, a little worse for the wear for all its decades and not very large, but cozy on the inside and perfectly suited for my friend's needs. Right now, it looked gray even in the sunlight, huddled in on itself. I rang the doorbell that was the newest thing on the front of the house and waited.

The door opened after a while and I saw Thomas looking out at me. His eyes caught my attention first; a complete opposite of how they had looked at the station, they were tired, weary, empty. As if there was nothing left to see in the world anymore. I had seen him in passing a few times since he returned, and he had looked tired to me then, but I hadn't realized the full extent of it until that look stared at me from the relative darkness of his door.

"William. Come in. Good to see you, I suppose."

I looked at him again as my eyes adjusted to the relative gloom. His cheeks were sunken, his face unshaven by a few days; I couldn't help but be reminded of Dr. House from the TV series, and his expression went right with that.

"Tom, how are you? Is everything well?"

He pondered this for a while and shrugged. It felt discouraging; as if he just didn't care whether he was well. He turned and beckoned me to follow him as he ambled to his study, where we had sat and talked before.

The lights were on here, but somehow it still looked gloomy. There was a faint, vague, unwashed smell in the room. Thomas sat down in his chair and offered me a drink from among what I observed was a rather larger collection than before of bottles of liquor, full and empty both. He noticed my glance.

"Yes, I do drink more than I used to. I'm not an alcoholic yet, but we'll have to see about that. Now sit down. How have you been, Bill?"

All this was said without much enthusiasm. I found myself answering in the same manner.

"Oh, fine, fine. You know, the usual."

"And how's the wife?"

"She's taken up oil painting. She seems to be having fun with it, so that's good, but I just hope she won't want to hang any of those paintings on our walls."

Thomas responded with the slightest smirk of amusement.

"But you know I didn't come here to talk about me," I went on. "What about you? Like I said on the phone, you haven't seemed yourself lately."

"Ha. Oh, I'm myself. It's the world that's different all of a sudden."

"I hadn't noticed," I said. "Would you like to enlighten

me?"

Thomas sighed and got up. He walked to the window and gazed up into the sky.

"You were certainly always one of my smarter friends. Remember those conversations we had sometimes? About the big questions. Life, the universe, and everything. God and morality. The meaning of life."

"Yes. Those conversations are always interesting, perhaps because there are no final answers to such questions."

I have never heard anything so sardonic as Thomas's small laugh at that point. "Oh, but you are wrong about that. We both were. Though you were more right. You had the answer all along."

"I don't follow."

"You will. You see, I know now. I have found out all of it. It was so simple. I never knew, but now I do."

He turned to look at me, a hint of intensity in his eyes again for a change, but all I could do was look back with polite puzzlement.

"I found out the answer. And it was your answer. It was... God all along."

For a moment, I thought I caught a glimpse of sense in what he was saying. The existence of God was something Thomas and I had always politely disagreed about. He saw no place or need for a higher being, seeing everything in terms of science, the world devoid of any ultimate purpose, though somehow that lack seemed not to bother him. For me, though I was skeptical of some of the teachings of the Christian church, it was natural to think in terms of a supreme being maintaining the order of the cosmos and looking after humanity. Our views had much else in common, but this difference was always at the bottom.

Yet, I was sure Thomas would not become depressed if he were to start believing in God.

Thomas sat down in front of me again. "Let me tell you what happened from the beginning."

Speaking as if the words felt unnatural in his mouth, he began:

"God spoke to me in a dream. I saw... the heavens, clouds like mountains, the unearthly shapes of angels, like great birds made of light. And I was faced with a presence so bright I could not perceive it, yet it filled all my senses. It was God, and He spoke to me."

"And... what did He say?"

"He said He wanted me to know He... was. He said He understood my disbelief, but it was time to end it. He said He... loved me and wanted me to know Him. And then, I woke up, feeling a sense of great joy and elation like I had never experienced in my life. Never."

"Many people have had experiences like this," I tried, "and those who do know that God has spoken to them, they can't prove it, but..."

"Oh, bah, I didn't believe then," he interrupted me crossly. "We've talked about this before, and I told you, even if I had one of those experiences myself, I wouldn't take it any more seriously, no matter how it felt. That wasn't all. When I had clearly awoken, still dazed by the experience, and, all right, feeling great, elevated, but not believing it was real at all... once I was fully awake, I heard God's voice again. 'I know you need proof,' He said, 'and you shall have proof.' And that was when this appeared, right in front of my eyes, out of nowhere."

Thomas turned around on his chair and opened his bottom left desk drawer. As he reached inside, I heard a brief intake of breath; looking at his eyes, I saw he was affected again, as if the mysterious "this" was too powerful not to upset him even in his current apathy.

Thomas's eyes went back to a bored, slightly irritated look again when he raised up the object and looked at it. He seemed to resent it.

"It was floating in the air," he explained. "As I reached out my hand and grasped it, I felt gravity take hold of it. Not all of it, obviously. It remained like this. Go on, take a look."

I reached out gingerly and took hold of the pedestal. I was not sure what I was seeing, so I held the object in front of me and studied it. After discerning its shape, I still had no idea what it was.

There was a small metal pedestal, a few centimeters high, an odd silvery white in color. Above it, there was a floating sphere with a smaller sphere orbiting around it slowly, made of the same material.

I carefully turned the system of objects around in my hands. The spheres turned with the pedestal; their relative positions remained the same, save for the smaller one continuing its orbital movement. I moved my fingers between the separate parts of the object. There was nothing but air, not even a tingle of electricity.

I don't know whether I studied the object for half a minute or five minutes. It was just baffling, vaguely upsetting, though hypnotically beautiful in its simplicity.

Then I remembered the context and looked up at

Thomas. He'd claimed this had appeared out of nowhere?

"Thomas, what is this?"

"A miracle!" he said bitterly. "An unquestionable, proven miracle, a violation of the laws of physics."

"But..."

"I didn't believe it easily, of course," he went on. "God told me to have it examined before He fell silent. I was feverish. You saw me at the station. This was something unbelievable, potentially earthshaking. Not that I believed right away, mind you! As extraordinary as it was either way, a hoax was still more likely. But this had some potential to finally be some real proof—not that I'd been expecting or waiting for that, but it opened new possibilities that had never been opened before. So I made arrangements and eventually managed to get someone at a physics lab to believe it would be worth their while to examine what I had.

"Well, I went there, and they took it just as I would have had them do, an interesting puzzle they would certainly solve. They thought about magnetism, of course, and were half convinced I'd made this thing myself. They studied it and couldn't figure it out. So they got even more scientists there, even some top names, and they all thought it was a jolly good puzzle, though most thought it wouldn't involve any physical principles they didn't know. And, well, they were right, weren't they? It's not based on any physical principles. It's a miracle.

"They kept on studying this thing and started to get more frustrated. Its chemical composition is nothing special, apparently, but the parts can't be brought apart and it can't be seriously damaged by any means, and there's absolutely no physical explanation for how it defies gravity. The spheres can't be removed from their place and the orbiting sphere can't be stopped from moving in relation to the rest with any amount of force. It'll go right through rock if it has to.

"Some of the scientists got angry, others were fascinated. They called in even more people, and no one could figure it out.

"And just when they'd officially admitted defeat, as it were, that's when it happened. I hadn't told them the whole truth about how I got this, because they'd have thought me crazy, and I'd resisted their interrogations. I just repeated I'd found it on my bedside and thought it was a prank. But now they could all see. We could all feel that sense of indescribable awe that I had felt in my dream. The ceiling of the room vanished and was replaced by a vision of heaven. And God spoke to all of us and said He had sent this miracle to prove Himself to me and other unbelievers present at the time."

I looked at the impossible object in my hands again, suddenly wanting to put it down to avoid some indefinable danger. "Are you really serious?"

"Look, believe me or not, I decided I'd tell you my story, so you'll damn well listen. I've never been as serious."

"All right. Go on..."

"Some of the scientists were atheists before that moment. Others weren't. But afterward, there was only one very angry man left among them who claimed still not to believe. It was ironic how irrational and emotional he acted. I mean, I'm used to thinking that's religious people who do that. But there was no rational barrier to belief at that point. We had all witnessed a miracle, as reliably as can be conceived, and we all felt the presence of God and sat at His foot as He instructed us in the secrets of being."

I stared at Thomas for a moment. Then I stared at the thing in my hands.

Thomas waved a hand. "Yes, sure, unbelievable. But suppose this is all true for the moment so that we can talk about it, and I can tell you everything."

"All right..." Perhaps I could make more sense of this after some questions. "So... did you... learn the secrets of existence?"

"Oh, yes." He almost spat this. "I understand... I know it all now. All the deepest questions. For example, do you want to know what the point of our existence is?"

"I... of course I would."

"The point of our existence, the purpose of human life, is to believe in God and love Him. That's all. In faith, it is fulfilled. As long as you keep faith, your purpose is fulfilled. So you, for example, you're already set. All you have to do is keep that faith for the rest of your life."

I stared down blankly for a moment.

"Well? Come on, you were all about the deep questions before."

I racked my brain for some of them. "So... I take it there is life after death as well?"

"Yes. Once we die, those who believed in God will spend an eternity in His presence in perfect happiness. Those who don't will deny themselves this and essentially cease to exist. Nothing in this life can compare to heaven, and once we are there, we will see all our past toils and sorrows as insignificant."

"But... that's wonderful, right?"

"Oh, yes," Thomas spat. "Nothing we do here matters save faith. Well, except of course that there are moral responsibilities. Do you want to know the secret of morality?"

"Well..."

"Morality is based on God's command. Forget all that stuff I used to say about how we need to agree on rules to get along and shouldn't harm each other just because we're all equally valuable. Sure, that's all true, but it's not the ground for morality. It could never be. Only God's command can be. We must do as God commands, and that's all there is to it.

"And we know God's commands based on our consciences. Usually, our minds are awfully muddled so we don't always know what's truly our inborn conscience talking. But me, I've looked upon the face of God, and now I hear His will clearly in my heart. I can always tell what's right. There isn't any rule that we can properly understand, but our conscience always tells us what's right.

"For example, abortion is sometimes right, but at some point, the unborn baby becomes a person and it's murder. The line goes at about two months. I can't give you a rule, but show me a particular case, and I'll know."

"You always agreed you can't draw exact lines like that," I ventured.

"Ha, well, my conscience was muddled then, wasn't it? I was trying to figure things out by myself, see what was right based on reason and experience. Well, none of that. Besides, it's quite clear when someone is a person or not. It starts when the soul enters the body. Oh, and you know what, there's another mystery solved. How can there be minds as well as matter? Well, you were right about that too, although it's even simpler. Mental properties exist besides physical ones because there are mental substances, which are our souls. Our souls control our physical brains without breaking natural laws through quantum fluctuations whose effects are strengthened by chaotic processes. I won't try to explain what that means. It's also how we have free will."

"What about the mind-body problem...?"

"The interaction happens because God says so. It's basically a miracle, though so is every other law of nature if you go there."

"So every law of nature...?"

"Exists because God decided it should. Go on, ask me more."

It's hard to express how different this was from our usual conversations, with their complicated twists and turns and different perspectives. But then again, if God Himself gave the answers to you, wouldn't it all finally be clear?

"So... why does the universe exist? Why is there something rather than nothing?"

"It exists so we can exist, so that God can love and be loved. Next."

"Umm... what about the problem of evil?"

"It's just an illusion. We shouldn't be trying to judge God based on our limited understanding. And remember morality is determined by God's command."

"So He can do whatever he likes?"

"Oh, no. He's omni-benevolent, after all. The objectively correct ethical theory is deontology, which means it's all about duties. God sets Himself a higher set of duties than to anyone else. And He fulfills them all completely, hence He's omni-benevolent. He couldn't be any more good, that's a meaningless idea. There's nothing beyond fulfilling all your duties."

"So what about all the suffering in the world?"

"It's not God's duty to end all suffering. The world would be a much more terrible place if He slacked on any of His duties, and we should be grateful, but that's not the point. The reasons we have to complain about the world being the way it is are all illusory. Actually, there is nothing left to morally demand of the world or of God, because God has done His duty perfectly. Anyway, if any of the suffering bothers you, remember that you just need to believe in God and wait a few decades and none of this will matter at all because you'll be perfectly happy for eternity."

"Are you saying this life has no point?"

"Absolutely not! I have it on the highest authority what the point of life is! It's to love and obey God. If I were talking about feeling like there's no point, or that there's some other point, I'd just be talking about my subjective feelings. This is the official point, embedded in the very nature of the universe."

Thomas fell silent. I stared at him quietly. He stared back gloomily.

It felt like half an hour, but in truth it was probably just a few minutes until I broke the silence.

"Thomas?"

"Yes."

"All of this... really?"

I stared him in the eye and put all the weight I could into that question.

He stared back at me and answered, in a level tone but with even more force.

"Yes."

I looked down and we were silent for another few minutes. I realized I was convinced he really did believe. I stared at the impossible object, and a chill went through me.

"I... think I understand," I said finally.

Thomas sighed deeply. "Really, Bill?"

"Yes. I... think so. Do you feel better now? Are you ready to stop this... isolation?"

I looked up at him for the first time just in time to see his shoulders sag.

"Then you don't understand. William, I... thanks for listening and being patient, but get the hell out of here now. No, I don't feel better, and clearly you can't help me one bit. I'm trying not to be too bitter, but I'm failing, so just shut up and get out."

* * *

I'm still trying to understand.

My life has not been radically changed like Thomas's was. I live on, go to work, meet friends, spend time with my family. I suppose something has changed. It's hard for me to attend to the deep questions anymore. I only think about the answers I heard. Of course, with Thomas hiding in his house in ever-deeper isolation, I don't have anyone much to talk with anyway. Somehow, though, they sometimes keep me awake at night—not the questions but these proposed answers.

And the last remaining big question—why did Thomas react like that?

I may have some inkling of the answer, buried somewhere in the back of my head, perhaps in a hidden part of me that thinks like Thomas. I don't know what it is, but I suspect it.

Because I still don't know whether I believe Thomas or not, though I believe he was sincere. And some part of me is glad

I don't know. If I accepted them, those answers would give me everything I wanted to know about the world on a deep level. At the same time, they would give me the confidence and trust I have gained from faith before.

But somehow, it feels as if, if I believed them, there would be nothing left. No, not that—not just nothing left to explore or no mystery to life. Something even deeper. Not the having of answers—I like understanding things—but having answers such as these. It's like staring into a void, except that I keep imagining it as a small, empty room instead of infinite blackness.

* * *

This story first appeared in the After Dinner Conversation—November 2020 issue.

Discussion Questions

1. If God spoke to you, as happened in the story to Thomas, would that be enough to cause you to believe in God? If not, what more would you need?

2. Thomas calls the object a "miracle" because it does not obey any known laws of physics. Do you agree? Is there some bit of technical information that would cause you to believe (*or not believe*) the object was a miracle?

3. Thomas asserts that nothing matters save faith. Does that answer create happiness, hope, sadness, or another emotion in you? Is it motivating or demotivating?

4. According to Thomas, the "mind-body problem" is solved because of God's miracle. He also has solutions for the "problem of evil" (*it's an illusion*) and the omni-benevolent vs. omni-powerful problem of God as outlined by Epicurus (*it's not God's duty to end suffering*). Are these answers sufficient for you?

5. What is the strongest and weakest evidence in the story to support Thomas's belief in God?

* * *

Sacrificing Mercy

Henry McFarland

* * *

<u>Content Disclosure</u>: Mild Language; Medical Procedures

* * *

Inwardly I raged against Jenny's religion, her God, and yes against her. She had a chance at life, at health. How could she refuse it? Damn the religion that told her to destroy our hope! But showing my rage would make it harder to persuade her. Besides, it was time to help her into bed. The doctor's visit had exhausted Jenny, and she quickly dropped off to sleep. She looked as peaceful as a saint in a stained-glass window and as fragile.

On a spring day ten years ago, a petite young woman with a pixie haircut pushed a shopping cart piled high with groceries across our college campus. Some cans fell from the top of the pile. I picked them up and offered to help push the cart. Jenny's bright blue eyes widened in a smile that lit up the world.

Jenny led me to the food pantry at a local church, where an obese woman with a loud cough sat on the stoop and puffed on a cigarette. Jenny sat next to the woman and said in a cheery voice, "Good morning Mrs. Simpson, I hope you feel better. Come on inside, we've got tomato soup—your favorite."

Mrs. Simpson might have been better off if she used the money she spent on cigarettes to buy her own soup. Still, something in Jenny's kindness to her touched me. Because of that, and to spend time with Jenny, I began to help in the food pantry—just one day a week. Soon my life revolved around Jenny. We married the week after graduation and settled down for a blissful four years of health.

Then came four years of sickness. Cardiomyopathy attacked her heart and began a deterioration that doctors could slow but never stop. I did what I could for her, including learning how to draw her blood for the tests that never found any hope. Nothing stopped the disease. Every halting step she took, every moan she made, every tear she shed reminded me of how helpless I was.

Only a new heart could save her, but the chance of that was slim. People who needed hearts far outnumbered the donors. The hospital put her on a waiting list, but she'd likely die waiting.

My one source of hope was a daily internet search for information on possible new treatments. Three years ago, there was something promising. I told Jenny about it as I drew her blood. "They just started trials on a way to grow a new heart."

"So that's why you looked so intense, like you wanted to jump inside your computer. How could they do that?"

"With stem cells from embryos that are clones of the patient."

Her eyes narrowed. "Cloning's unnatural."

Nature wasn't helping us much. "It's a way to get a new heart without waiting for a donor." I swabbed a spot on her arm with alcohol. Her flesh once had a rosy glow—now it was almost blue. "You'll just feel a little pinch now."

"You're always so gentle. Mike, what happens to the baby?"

"Baby?"

Her eyes got narrower, her forehead wrinkled. "The embryo, what happens to her?"

"Don't know. Maybe they won't have to use an embryo."

As the disease progressed, Jenny's life seemed to shrink. One by one she had to give up the activities she loved. Her worst moment was when the doctor said that she could no longer teach. She wept on our way home after that appointment, and her hands clutched the cross she wore around her neck. At home, we embraced on the sofa, and she poured out her sorrow and frustration.

"I feel so useless."

"Jenny, no, you still mean the world to me."

"I can't work. I can't help around the house. I can't even be a wife to you anymore."

I was all too aware of that last loss, but I didn't want that to show. "You're the woman I love, and don't you ever forget it. You aren't useless."

Jenny hugged me tighter. "I love you too, Mike. I must have faith. God has a reason for all this."

I didn't say anything about God's reasons. Soon after we'd started dating, Jenny gave me her big open smile and asked me to go to church with her that Sunday. At Calvary Evangelical, the congregation gathered in a large undistinguished space with a high ceiling, like the waiting room in a train station but with an altar and pews. Nothing hung on the walls but a large cross. During the service, she stared at the altar with a wide-eyed fascination. I was mildly interested, or maybe less than mildly. Luckily it only took an hour.

As we left, Jenny gave a little laugh. "At least you didn't fall asleep. That's a start."

Time to be positive. "I liked the choir."

She hugged me. "You're a good person, Mike. Keep coming to church. You'll get it."

I didn't get it. Jenny wanted me to go to church, so I did, but with no real conviction. For hope I looked to research, not to heaven.

* * *

Now research could save us. The trials were over, and the method worked. Dozens of patients had gotten newly grown hearts. Jenny had a chance, and I brought her to Dr. Yifang Phang to take that chance.

The doctor explained the procedure. "All we need now are some cells from your body—a blood sample will do fine. We can use that to start the cloning."

Jenny's voice was weak but clear. "What happens to the baby?"

Dr. Phang took a deep breath. "You mean the blastocyst? It would not be viable after the stem cells were extracted."

"So you'd kill her."

Dr. Phang sounded as if she were reading a script. "Some would feel that way. Others would question whether a blastocyst, that's what I prefer to call an embryo at such an early stage, would really be a baby."

Jenny leaned forward. Her eyes were fixed on Phang. "Whatever you call the embryo, it's a human life at its earliest stage, when it's most helpless, most vulnerable."

"Not all share your point of view. Also, the process here is not similar to the typical process that results in the birth of a baby. The blastocyst would be formed by somatic nuclear cell transfer, not the union of a sperm and egg."

Jenny paused for a moment. "Is there any other way to get the stem cells?"

Phang shook her head. "Not for this procedure. It requires embryonic stem cells because of their greater pluripotency, their ability to become other types of cells. In a few years, we may be able to use other types of stem cells. But Mrs. Thompson, you don't have that time. Without a new heart, you won't live more than a few months."

Jenny sighed. "Could we do something else instead?"

"This new procedure is the only way to get a heart. There's no real chance of an old-fashioned transplant with a donor heart. Now that we've developed this new technology, getting donor organs has gone from hard to almost impossible. No one thinks of donating organs when new organs can be grown instead. Besides insurance wouldn't cover it."

That surprised me. We hadn't had an insurance problem before. "Why not?"

Phang gave me a sympathetic look. "Because the heart wouldn't have the recipient's own genetic makeup, the patient would need lifetime treatment with antirejection drugs. Those drugs are very expensive and often have serious side effects. Because it's so much more expensive than using an organ cloned from the patient, the insurance companies won't pay. The cost is well over two million, not including the antirejection drugs post-transplant."

That we could never afford.

"Doctor, I can't have this procedure." Jenny sounded so calm.

I reached over and touched her hand. "Jenny, this could save you."

She turned to me. "I'm sorry, Mike. But this procedure is wrong. I can't do it. I don't fear my death."

I feared her death! Without her I'd be alone. I felt nauseous. We'd been on a long journey, and with the destination finally in sight, she refused to move. Phang was the specialist. Couldn't she say something to change Jenny's mind?

Phang's voice showed no emotion. "Then all I can do is continue palliative care. You should sign a living will. Also, you'll need a medical power of attorney. You're likely to go into a coma before you die, and you should designate someone to make decisions for you during that time." She gave us the paperwork, and Jenny left the office with me trailing behind.

The next night, Jenny, her breathing slow and labored, lay in bed. I sat next to her and took her hands in mine. "Please darling, have the procedure. I need you, to have you near me, to hold you."

Jenny sounded regretful but adamant. "Mike, I love you so much. Please try to understand. The procedure goes against my beliefs."

"If you have this procedure, you can have your life back. You can teach again. Once you told me that poor people shouldn't be denied medical care. How can you deny yourself medical care?"

Jenny began to cry a little. "Mike, I don't want to die. But do you remember in my second year of teaching when that little boy Bryan died of cancer?"

"You cried all night."

"I did, but that taught me that yes, bad things happen, and we don't know why God lets them happen or what his plan is. But we always have God's loving presence in our lives, and that presence gives our lives meaning. To find that meaning, we must follow God's laws. There's no true hope in going against those laws."

I stroked her hand as she dropped off to sleep. Jenny had spoken from an inner strength. Perhaps I should have admired that. I couldn't.

* * *

Jenny's mom came over a couple of days later. Esther Davis was a quiet, diminutive woman in her early fifties. We weren't close, but we got along. Jenny told her mother everything, so Esther knew about her daughter's refusal and its consequences. Esther was as religious as Jenny. What side would she be on?

The three of us sat on the sofa with Jenny in the middle. Esther shook her head no to my offer of tea or soda. She fixed her eyes on her daughter. "Jenny, I've been thinking about the procedure and praying about it, and I believe you should have it."

Jenny's eyes widened. "I've prayed about it too, Mom, and I've talked to the pastor about it. I can't do it."

"Jenny, Jesus says, 'I desire mercy, not sacrifice.' You're only twenty-nine—if you don't have this procedure, there's no other hope."

Jenny reached over and touched her mother's hand. "There is, there's always hope in God."

"Please Jenny," Esther pleaded, "Jesus wouldn't want my baby to die."

"Jesus teaches us that sometimes we must suffer for our faith. The early martyrs knew that."

"What about Mike? You'll be leaving him all alone."

Jenny kept looking at her mother, not at me. "I know it's hard on Mike. I know, but..."

Esther began to sob. "You don't know how hard. You don't know how hard it is to lose the one you married. I'd have done anything to save your father."

Jenny sounded sympathetic but unmoved. "Jesus comforted you when Dad died. Jesus will comfort Mike too."

I kept silent, not saying the comfort I wanted was health for Jenny.

Esther moved closer to her daughter and put her arms around her. "Jenny, you're my only child. Please promise that you'll continue to think about the procedure and pray about it. I love you, and God loves you too. He wants you to live."

Jenny hesitated. "I'll still pray about it. But I have to follow the Lord." She bowed her head for a moment. "I have to rest now, Mom."

Jenny watched through the window as Esther's lonely, stooped figure walked to her car. Then she sighed and went up to bed.

The next evening, Jenny sat next to me on the sofa and took my hand in hers. "Mike, I have to give someone a medical power of attorney. It has to be someone who'll respect my wishes." She stared up at me with big eyes the pale blue of the early morning sky. "Can I trust you to do that?"

We were preparing for when she would slip away from me and into a coma.

Jenny went on talking. "At first, I planned to ask Mom to do it, but it might be too hard for her. Can you make sure only good things are done?"

I looked her in the eyes. "Yes. Yes I can, and I will." I embraced her and rubbed my hands over her back. I hoped I'd find the courage for what I knew I had to do.

* * *

Dr. Phang and I met in her office, where nothing hung on the walls but her medical degree. She leaned back in her chair. "Mike, growing a new heart takes time. If we're going to do it, we have to start now."

"Jenny's still against it."

Her voice softened. "I'd been hoping that she'd change her mind. But if she won't, we'll have to talk about end-of-life care."

"Suppose you developed a heart from someone else's cells. That would solve the problem of not having a donor heart, wouldn't it?"

"Yes, but the patient would still need antirejection drugs, so insurance wouldn't cover it."

I already knew that. "Just growing the heart itself isn't too costly, is it?"

"That alone no, but what's the point of doing that if you can't use the heart?"

"How much would it cost for everything up to the operation?"

She gave me a *why do you want to know that* look. "First

there'd be the compatibility tests on the DNA. Those are about $5,000. Then there'd be the growth of the blastocyst, the harvesting of the stem cells, and the growth of the heart. That would be about $25,000."

"Could you postpone the compatibility tests until after the heart is grown? If I can't use it, I don't want to pay for more than necessary."

She hesitated for a moment. "Yes, we could do that. The tests don't take long, and they don't have to be done until just before the operation."

I drew a small vial of blood from my pocket and put it on the desk in front of her. "This is my blood. My wife won't agree to using her cells in cloning, but you can use mine. Grow a new heart from my cells."

"Wouldn't your wife still object—it would involve embryonic stem cells?"

"Maybe she'll change her mind. You make sure that if she does, there's a heart for her."

"What about the cost of the operation and the antirejection drugs?"

"My worries, not yours."

She looked at the blood. Then she looked at me the way a TV cop looks at a suspect. "You realize, Mr. Thompson, that the law has serious penalties for using someone's cells in cloning without their permission."

"So what? They're my cells, and you have my permission."

"You're sure?"

I tried to sound irritated, the way someone who was telling the truth would sound. It's especially important to sound truthful when you're lying. "I know when my blood is drawn. If you want me to sign something, I will." I signed a lot of forms and left her with the blood.

Jenny's life faded like a picture left in the desert sun. Eventually, she lapsed into a coma, and they took her to the hospital. Dr. Phang met me in a small conference room near the emergency room. "I'm very sorry about your wife's condition, Mr. Thompson, but we do need to discuss how to care for her."

"Doctor, take the heart grown from the blood sample I gave you and transplant it into her body."

The doctor looked grave. "As the heart was based on your cells, I can't transplant it without first preparing your wife with antirejection drugs. That would—"

"You won't need any antirejection drugs. That was her blood, and the heart is genetically hers."

"You told me that it was your blood. She didn't authorize using her blood." Her voice showed no emotion.

"What do you care? I told you in writing that it was my blood. You're off the hook, aren't you?" She opened her mouth to speak, but I kept talking. "All that matters now is you have a heart that matches her genetically. I have medical power of attorney, and that gives me the right to make treatment decisions for my wife. I'm making that decision. Give her the cloned heart."

"I have to report the unauthorized cloning."

"Go ahead. You can't be blamed for cloning the heart, and you'll face no consequences for it." I waited a second, then went on. "If my wife dies because you refused her a legally authorized treatment, that'd have consequences."

They let me see Jenny after the surgery. She looked tiny

and frail as she lay in a large bed with tubes running into her body and monitor screens all around her. But she lived.

In a few days, Dr. Phang thought Jenny was well enough to be told why a healthy heart now beat inside her. When the doctor finished her explanation, Jenny turned on me. "You knew I didn't want this! You betrayed me."

"Jenny, it was the only way to save you."

"You haven't saved me! Leave me alone now, please." She turned her face to the pillow and began to sob.

Dr. Phang touched my arm and suggested that I leave.

Four days later, her nurse called to say that Jenny wanted to see me.

She sat up in her hospital bed. Color had returned to her cheeks, and her eyes were bright. She was like a flower that was blooming again, but her eyes bored into me. "Mike, I can't accept what you did."

"I needed you to live. I wanted to have you—"

"Yes, you needed, you wanted. You didn't do it for me. You did it for yourself."

"Darling, you wouldn't be alive if I hadn't done it."

"You don't understand. I'd wondered for so long—I knew God has a reason for my suffering, but I didn't know what it was. Finally, I realized that the Lord allowed my sickness to happen because by refusing the treatment, I could show others how wrong the treatment is. My suffering could have had a purpose, but you destroyed that."

Could I make her understand? "Your suffering showed that you needed help, and I got it for you."

Jenny's voice softened. "You didn't help me. My life was based on principles. That's what gave it meaning. Now I must live a life that comes from betraying those principles, a life that's been forced on me. Can you at least tell me you realize what you did was wrong?"

I took a long deep breath. "Saving you wasn't wrong."

Tears began to run down Jenny's cheeks. "Then we can't be together, Mike. Please leave now."

* * *

I had to spend only four months in prison, a chance to get a lot of exercise and read a lot of books. The hardest part was knowing that when I'd be released, Jenny wouldn't be there.

One day they brought me up to the visitors' room. Dirt had turned the white walls a light gray, and the air reeked of unwashed flesh. Dozens of voices filled the room with a throbbing sound. Esther sat there braving it all. "Mike, I want to thank you for saving my daughter's life. I told her that Jesus who called Lazarus from the grave would bless what you've done."

"How is Jenny?"

Esther smiled. "She's a lot better. She's going to teach kindergarten this fall."

"That's so great."

Esther's hands moved closer to me. Perhaps she would have hugged me, had prison rules allowed it. "Mike, she feels hard against it now, but I'm praying that Jenny will forgive you and that you and she will reconcile."

"Thank you so much, Esther." How could reconciliation be possible? Jenny would never accept what I'd done. I'd never say it was wrong.

When I was released, they found me a new job and a small apartment. Its bare walls kept saying Jenny wasn't there. One day I walked past her school. The kindergartners were playing in the school yard, and a little boy fell down and began to sniffle. Jenny went to him. She was as quick and light on her feet as before the sickness. She comforted the boy then sent him off to bravely rejoin the game. I didn't let her see me. She wouldn't want her ex-con ex-husband hanging around.

Later I passed a large red brick church and decided to go inside. The church was much more ornate than the one Jenny attended. Sunlight streamed through stained-glass windows and filled the space with color. I knelt before a mural of a robed figure with long hair and a beard and prayed to the God who had called Lazarus from the grave.

* * *

This story first appeared in the After Dinner Conversation—October 2020 issue.

Discussion Questions

1. Do you respect Jenny's decision to refuse treatment? Would you refuse treatment if you were in her shoes? Is your opinion different, knowing that the blastocyst that would be destroyed would be just a few hundred cells?

2. Is Jenny being selfish to others by refusing treatment based on her religious values? Would she be selfish if her religious values caused her to refuse more common treatment, like a blood transfusion or taking antibiotics?

3. Even if the husband disagreed with Jenny's decision, did he have a duty to honor her wishes? Did Jenny have a duty to divorce him after she found out what he had done?

4. Is a person's sense of honor, duty, and/or faith more important than their life? Is a person's first duty always to their life? Why or why not?

5. Jenny says, *"I realized that the Lord allowed my sickness to happen because by refusing the treatment, I could show others how wrong the treatment is. My suffering could have had a purpose, but you destroyed that."* Is Jenny correct, given that she didn't personally accept treatment? Does it matter that, even if she died, practically no one would have known she refused treatment, or is the symbolism of the refusal the important thing?

* * *

In Their Image

Abra Staffin-Wiebe

* * *

<u>Content Disclosure</u>: Mild Violence

* * *

When I stepped off the shuttle and breathed in the dry grass scent of Trade City, I was still confident I could launch the first human church on Landry's World. My fellow passengers had been politely uninterested when I explained the mission my church had sent me on. A few had shaken their heads as they glided away. I thought maybe they objected to a female preacher. Or maybe it was because I'm an ex-marine. I'm an "ex-" lot of things: ex-marine, ex-atheist, ex-drunk, ex-wife, and ex-mother—that last because I was a poor enough mother that when my kids grew up, they washed their hands of me.

The heavier gravity made my normal stride more of a shuffle, but my spirits were high as I walked to meet the young woman waiting for me. After all, I was here at the request of Amber Sands Mining, the major human employer on the planet. The indigenous government had approved; they even volunteered the labor to build my church. My denomination's elders were delighted to have finally found a mission suitable for an ex-marine with other-world experience.

My guide held a sign saying, "Preacher." She bestowed a chipper smile on me when I approached. "Welcome to Landry's World! I'll take you directly to the church so that you can get started."

As I fell into step beside her, I said, "It seems odd that a planet with indigenous life is named after the captain who discovered it. Discovered isn't quite the right term, either, is it?"

"Landry's purpose in life was to find and name this world, and the Teddies honor that."

I raised my eyebrows. "Teddies?"

"Oh, dear. I hope you didn't memorize their long-form name! You don't need to worry about that. We need to say that in the welcome packet."

I remembered the images that had come with my briefing. The locals of Landry's World were seven feet tall, ursine, and covered in bright pink fur. "Wait. You're telling me that this place is populated by pink teddy bears?" I asked incredulously.

She grinned. "Yup. Here's the road. Watch your step. I thought we could walk instead of taking the transit tube."

The golden sand between the borders of the road appeared identical to the sand that stretched into the distance on either side. "What's the difference?"

"Everything in its place."

"And what's your place? When you're not shepherding green recruits, I mean?"

"This is my place."

"Of course, but this can't take up all your time. I meant, what else do you do? What are your plans for the future?"

"This is what I do," she answered stiffly.

A few failed attempts at conversation later, I let silence fall between us until she stopped in front of a crystalline three-story castle. Sunlight danced across jutting, sharp-edged planes of glass. A Teddy the color of raspberry sherbet rose from the shadow of the building. I'd been so dazzled that I hadn't even noticed him.

"Greetings," he said. "I am Soloulsoquebalso."

"Hello," I said.

"I am a Helper," he said, his fur emanating a neutral lemony scent. "Before taking up our Purpose, the youth of our church go out into the world and help others. I am to help you."

"But what are you doing—oh. This is the church your people built for us, isn't it?"

"It is suiting your Purpose?"

"It's beautiful." He still waited for my answer. "Yes, it will do very well. Would you like to attend my first service, this Sunday morning?"

He cocked his head. "You preach to us as well as to humans? This is part of your Purpose?"

"Well, yes."

A cotton candy scent rose from his fur. "I will help."

* * *

I expected to see him that Sunday, but there was only one Teddy in my congregation, and he was much too large to be Soloulsoquebalso. The Teddy sat in the front pew, beside five humans. They were the only ones in the whole church. I had expected a full house, from curiosity if nothing else. I gave the sermon my best, but as soon as I was done, they left without a word. They did not return the next Sunday. Instead, a different group of five humans—and one Teddy—sat in the front row.

That set the pattern. Humans from other stars occasionally attended my services when they passed through Trade City. Sometimes a drunk would stagger into the church and fall asleep in the pews. But mostly, I preached to the front row. I sweated bullets over my sermons, but I'll be the first to admit that I'm not a world-class orator.

I tried going out and inviting individual Teddies to attend. All I got were polite refusals. I tried asking humans. All they'd say was that they didn't need my church. When I asked why, they all said that I didn't need to know, that I was already doing what I was meant to. It sure didn't feel that way to me.

I was not totally surprised when I got a message saying that the Church Council had sent a delegation to discuss my mission's future.

* * *

I met them at Tamir's Café, the most Earthly—and expensive—restaurant on Landry's World. Instead of the omnipresent glass, Tamir had built the restaurant from blocks of a local rock that resembled the golden sandstone of his native Morocco. He pressed and varnished layers of lichen to achieve a homelike wood grain for his furniture. He filtered the air to remove the prevalent dry grass scent. Even the windows didn't reveal an alien landscape—synchronized holos showed a bustling Moroccan marketplace.

Under other circumstances, I would have eaten heartily. Today, I only ordered a bowl of harira. A fragrant cloud of ginger, pepper, and cinnamon rose from the soup, but I had to force myself to swallow even a few spoonfuls. The cause of my indigestion was the pair of elders sitting across the lovely false-wood table.

If they thought I had failed here on Landry's World, where would they send me? The Church was my only home now. My time as a pastor-in-training had already taught me that I didn't work well with others, no matter how much earnest goodwill existed on both sides. I'd lost the knack somewhere between the end of my stint as a marine and the beginning of my new life as an ex-alcoholic.

We made desultory conversation over dinner. I wasn't much for small talk, and dancing around the pachyderm in the room exhausted me. Elder Baldini seemed to be of like mind. Elder Velis filled our silences by chirping about the tourist attractions on Landry's World. When that failed, she told me all about the latest accomplishments of her grandchildren, whom I had never met.

Finally, she pushed back her plate. Her little-old-lady fluffiness vanished as the conversation got to business at last. "The Council sent us in person, in case you need spiritual counsel after hearing their decision."

Dread tightened my throat. "Yes?"

Elder Baldini hadn't participated much in the polite over-dinner small talk, but now he spoke. "It's not as grim as she makes it sound. It's only a budgetary readjustment. The mining company provided the initial funding for a church here on the recommendation of their human resources and morale department, but it seems that the... lack of interest... has changed their plans. Since most of the humans prefer the Teddy church services—"

"Excuse me?" I interrupted.

"Oh, didn't you know? Odd. They weren't at all reticent in discussing it with us. You could go to a service, see for yourself."

Elder Velis laid her hand on top of his, silencing him. "We aren't here to assign blame," she said. "I'm afraid the new budget will also have to cover your stipend, should you choose to remain." The figure she named erased my half-formed plans for a grand outreach program.

I didn't seriously consider leaving. From her tone, I guessed that if I left because the budget wasn't to my liking, the Church would not provide me with another pastoral post. Where else could I go?

"I may be able to assist with budgeting," Elder Baldini offered. "I was a practicing accountant for many years."

"Not—right now," I said. "I need to think." In truth, there was not much to think about. I knew my church's expenses as well as I knew my own. There would be enough, barely. If I was not extravagant in my wardrobe or my meals, I might be able to save a little for a maintenance fund. The cleaning service would have to go. It would hardly be the first time I'd scrubbed a floor. Some might say that was a waste of time, that I should be spending writing sermons, but washing floors also served God, even if it was a bit more Martha than Mary.

Elder Baldini nodded his understanding. Elder Velis asked our waiter for the bill and two containers for her leftovers and mine.

Although I rose with the elders and held the restaurant door open for them as we left, my actions were perfunctory. I remained lost in thought until Elder Velis stopped so suddenly that I almost walked into her.

"Here you go." She handed her leftovers to a beggar leaning against the wall.

I felt a flush of shame. I had grown too accustomed to the Teddies' habitually callous treatment of those less fortunate. I hadn't even seen the beggar until Elder Velis stopped. There was a sermon there, I thought, maybe even something good enough to keep people coming back.

Once I returned to my parsonage, I heated up the soup and retreated to my study. I was hyperaware of the bottom left-hand drawer of my desk, as if it radiated a heat that I could feel. That was where I kept an old bottle of Four Roses bourbon, never opened. The gesture had appealed to me when I saw it in an old 2D detective movie.

I jerked the drawer open, grabbed the bottle by the neck, and strode to the front door. Standing in the threshold, I threw the bottle out into the street. I expected the bottle to break. It bounced. I slammed the door shut on temptation and returned to my study.

As I sipped my cooling soup, I considered how I might write a sermon that would bring in the people who preferred— what?

How had Elder Baldini put it? That I could go and visit a Teddy service for myself? Very well. I might not need his accounting advice, but when it came to my failing church, I resolved that I would take all the help I could get.

* * *

I went to the Teddy church service the very next day, determined to find out what they offered that I did not. I arrived early and sat in the back, watching as bubblegum-furred Teddies lumbered in. One of them paused by my pew—a shining glass thing that managed to be far more comfortable than it appeared—and stared at me. Its brow wrinkled in the way that is their equivalent of a human grimace, and its scent sharpened. I thought it would speak to me then, but another wave of Teddies poured into the church and swept it along with them. Humans came, too. I felt a pang as I recognized some of the people who had attended one—and only one—of my services.

At the front of the church, facing the congregation, sat three Teddies with the strawberry-cheesecake-colored fur of the very old. I decided to think of them as the deacons.

When the church was packed with Teddies and humans, a new mother herded her tumble of pups to the front of the congregation to be welcomed. I smiled involuntarily at the sight of their big excited eyes and puffed-up hot pink fur. I saw the other humans also smiling, and a cotton candy scent of happiness and welcome rose from the congregation. Despite the ruthless savagery they exhibit in battle, Teddy parents are some of the most devoted I've seen on any planet. Every child is cherished. They even extend this across species lines. In the dry goods store, I once observed a stray child collect a gaggle of concerned Teddies who guarded her until she toddled back to her father.

After the welcome, the deacons rose to preach. They spoke in turns, seamlessly completing each other's sentences. It was a good trick, I admitted, but hardly one I could replicate.

Once I adjusted to the deacons' manner of speaking, I found their message—bland. There were no reminders of what God wanted, no exhortations to strive to become better, no celebrations of challenges met. They mouthed the same pablum

I'd heard a million times from commercial megachurches and feel-good inspirational speakers. Be the best you that you can be! Accept yourself! Be happy in who you are! Don't change because of what others consider good! Your flaws are who you are, and God needs you to be who you are! They were speaking Teddish, so I shifted dialects on my ear-cuff translator a few times to be sure I wasn't missing any nuances. I wasn't.

Of course, the Teddies added their own alien twist. As I listened, I learned that they believed there was no God—yet. We were God's attempt to create itself. The imminent God could only become real when we all became fully the thing that we were, when we achieved Purpose. God is made of many parts, the Teddies said, and only when all the parts simultaneously achieve Purpose will God arise. Those who turn aside from their Purpose, or who cannot find it, are reincarnated as another part of God, with another chance to achieve Purpose, until all the parts of God are aligned. When the deacons made this point, a low hum of affirmation rose from the audience.

"Remember," the deacons said, "true fulfillment is in keeping constant to your Purpose until the end. Choose rather to forsake your life than your Purpose."

As I listened, the Teddies' sweet scent grew strong and incense-like, an odor of sanctity that soothed me against my will. The deacons' words rolled through me. A part of me wished that I could relax into them, that I could believe God only wanted me to be a failed preacher to a tiny congregation, that I needn't struggle to change, that it would do no harm if I found that bottle of bourbon...

I pushed myself to my feet and stumbled away from the tranquilized audience. As soon as the doors retracted to allow me into the hallway, my head began to clear. Now I understood the appeal of the Teddies' preaching, but it was wrong. We could only be purified of our sins if we repented. True repentance is impossible without a change of mind, of heart, and of action. Clinging to "who you are" is clinging to the grave clothes of sin.

I walked down the hall until I came to a darkened, unoccupied room with a holo of a fish tank along one wall and a long couch facing it. A painted wall screen separated the room from another shadowed chamber beyond it. If I saw a similar place in a human church, I would call it a meditation room. Perhaps it served the same function for the Teddies. I stepped inside, sank into the embrace of the couch, and let my eyes follow the flickers of color in the tank as my mind wrestled with what I'd heard. My profession called me to love my enemies instead of shoot at them, so how could I fight the Teddies' doctrine?

I watched the darting, iridescent fish, at first absently and then with growing wonder. They were not holos after all. I rose, walked over to the tank, and tapped it with my fingernail. A gleaming fish swam over to investigate. An incredulous smile spread across my face. Fish were one of the few Earth species allowed on Landry's World, since they were small, portable, and easy to prevent from contaminating the ecosystem, but they were terribly expensive. One fish cost as much as a month's bar tab. People who needed a touch of Earth mostly made do with holos.

I could have stood there for hours, but in the room on the other side of the painted wall screen, someone turned on a light. I crept over to peer around the edge of the screen.

Four Teddies entered the room. I felt an itch of guilt over

my spying. Yet I did not look away. I found it difficult to tell Teddies apart, but I recognized the oldest as being one of the deacons. The smallest one I had not seen before, and the other two I was not certain about. They may have come from the church service, but the odor of sanctity had faded from their fur. I caught a whiff of an acrid burnt smell as the smallest one passed me. He lay on a peculiar, downward-tilted glass table with sides that cupped his body. Behind his head, the table formed a funnel that emptied into a large glass bowl, rather like a fishbowl.

What earthly—or *un*-Earthly—purpose could such a table serve? I was still pondering that when the deacon removed a dagger from one of his belt pouches and stabbed the smallest Teddy in the throat.

It was like seeing your childhood teddy bear sprout claws. As soon as I saw the blood, I snapped back into the heightened, battle-ready state that I thought I'd left behind forever when I went from soldier to minister. My mind raced through my options: escape, evade, report. But report what? To whom? What alien rite was I witnessing?

The small Teddy didn't try to defend himself. He never even raised a hand. Tremors shook his body for a minute or so. Then he lay still. A thin trickle of blackish-red blood ran down the inside of the glass table and dripped into the fishbowl whose purpose I had been wondering about. The deacon pulled the blade out with a horrible sucking sound, and more blood gurgled down the funnel.

The two remaining Teddies acted as if nothing had happened. One opened a large book whose paragraphs were etched on plates of glass, and the other took out what resembled a pair of pruning shears.

The Teddy holding the glass-plated book began to read. "True fulfillment is in keeping constant to your Purpose to the end. Choose rather to forsake your life than your Purpose. Let returning to your pieces remind you that God, too, is in pieces that only we can bring together. We can only make God in our image when we are aligned correctly. May the wheel of incarnation bring you around to the part of God that you are meant to be. These are the Purposes that we have known and recorded: hunter, warrior, soldier, baker, mother, tactician, fisher, planter of grain, collector of wild nuts, breeder of mukta, herder, diplomat..."

The other two Teddies bent over the corpse of their brother, tools in hand. The crunch of separating cartilage and bone carried clearly to my hiding spot behind the wall screen. My gorge rose, and I turned my head to the side. Witnessing this mutilation hit me as hard as anything I'd seen in the last war.

A patter of tiny paws drew my attention back instantly. A little pink puffball scampered in the door and froze, blinking at the horrific tableau in front of it. "What are you doing?" the pup asked.

"We are holding a funeral," the deacon told the pup. "This poor soul was unable to find Purpose, and so we are helping him back onto the wheel."

The pup blinked its big eyes. "Oh. Like Mother's sister's husband's brother."

"That's right, child. Now go back to your mother. She must be looking for you." The deacon stooped and patted the pup's back, shepherding it out of the room.

As it bounded away, I saw that the contact had left a

bloody handprint on the pup's fur.

I don't remember deciding that I had to leave. I don't remember walking out of the Teddies' church. I think I would have fought if anyone had tried to stop me, but the police never came for me, so I guess nobody did.

I was out of sight of the church when I noticed that I was being followed. When I glanced in a window, I caught a glimpse of a pink-furred Teddy trailing behind me. I turned a corner. He followed. I zigged across the street and took a shortcut through an alley. He followed. I stopped in front of a shop window and studied my pursuer while pretending interest in the array of mining respirators for sale.

Unlike a human stalker would have, the Teddy didn't stop. He lumbered right up to me. I tensed.

"Reverend," he rumbled, "mining equipment is not fitting to your Purpose. Why are you not at your church?"

I pretended he hadn't spoken. I didn't think I could interact politely with a Teddy just then.

"Why did you go to our service, Reverend?" he persisted. "You should be in your own church."

"That is no business of yours," I said sharply, turning and walking away.

"It is," he insisted, trotting after me. "I am to help you maintain Purpose."

After seeing what their obsession with Purpose caused, I couldn't respond to him in a way befitting a woman of God. I kept my back to the Teddy, kept walking, and tried to calm myself.

He followed me all the way across town to my church. He would have followed me into my study if I hadn't closed the door in his face. I tried working on my sermons, but all I could think of was the alien "funeral" I'd witnessed. Poor child, I thought, and I wasn't sure to whom I referred. A real preacher would have found inspiration in those memories, but all I found was anger and frustration. After several hours, I decided to abandon my study. Perhaps I could think more clearly outside.

When I opened my study door, I almost walked into a wall of pink fur. The Teddy had been sitting against the door, waiting, all this time. I stepped around him. His claws scrabbled against the floor as he pushed himself up to follow me.

I sat on a bench in the area that the landscaper had turned into a meditation garden. He had transformed a bare patch of alien land into something humans could find restful. Spindly shrubs, explosions of toadstools, and ruffled patches of lichen created patterns that pleased the eye. Purple grass grew in hummocks that rustled even when there was no breeze. Curving paths of sand soothed the soul. Since I had canceled the service that handled the church's cleaning and yard work, I supposed I would be the one who kept the paths swept and the grass trimmed from now on.

The Teddy sat beside me on the bench. His fur emanated a neutral lemony scent.

I could ignore him no longer. "Why are you following me?" I demanded.

"We were concerned when you left your church to attend ours. Then you went to a shop selling mining equipment. Those actions are not in line with your Purpose."

"You presume to know my purpose?"

"You are a woman of God, a preacher."

Well, he had me there. I switched tactics. "My actions are

no business of yours!"

"I am a Helper," he said. "I am to help you. Why did you go to our church service?"

"Why do you care?"

"All thinking beings are parts of God, and all must achieve Purpose to create God."

The thought of humans accepting this idea of Purpose made me sick. Would the Teddies kill us if we failed in our Purpose? What could I do about it?

"If I answer you, will you leave me alone?" I snapped.

"If you no longer need help."

"I went to observe the competition."

"Why did you walk through the town instead of taking a transit tube back to your church? Why were you studying objects belonging to other Purposes?"

"I walked because I needed to clear my head. I witnessed your church forcing one of its own to the slaughter. You call it a funeral, I believe."

"Force—no! When he realized he had no Purpose, he went to our elders and asked for his funeral. Reincarnation and a new Purpose was his only hope of salvation."

"You say that like you think it was a good decision."

"It is the only possible one."

"You would do the same if you had no Purpose?"

"Of course."

"So what is your Purpose, then?" I demanded.

He took some time to answer me, and I decided that the bitter-orange scent suddenly in the air must indicate embarrassment. "I have not found it yet. Many youths have not."

"Many?" I asked.

He curved his body away from me. "A few."

I took his response as a victory and settled back to enjoy the peace. Eventually, I sighed. "You're not leaving, are you?"

"No."

"Did you meet me at my church when I first arrived? Was that you?"

"Yes."

"I can't remember your name. Sol-something? If you're going to stick around, tell me what it is, so I know who to curse at," I said wryly.

A faint smell of burnt toast floated into the air. "Cursing is not fitting to your—"

I hurried to interrupt him. "I was joking! A sense of humor is a necessary thing for a preacher to have, I assure you."

The burnt smell faded. "I am Soloulsoquebalso."

"Right, then. I'll call you Saul."

Saul became my constant companion. If I shut him out of a room, he knocked politely on the door until I opened it. If I tried to slip away, he found me and asked urgently why I was leaving the church and abandoning my Purpose. Eventually, I gave up trying to escape. I grew accustomed to him, much as a soldier might grow accustomed to a large, furry, bright pink armchair if it were standard issue on base.

A few days after our first conversation, I returned to the meditation garden to make notes for my sermon. I was trying to figure out a way to say, "Stay away from the Teddies' church because they're murderous monsters," while still following the Bible's orders. It was uphill work. I'd signed up to love my enemies, to be kind and compassionate, and to minister to all races and peoples. Sure, nobody mentioned aliens, but I wasn't going to act like a barracks lawyer when it came to God's word.

I sighed as I set my notes on the bench beside me. I leaned back and closed my eyes. A soft swishing noise made me open them again. A strange Teddy was in my garden—sweeping. I watched, my mouth hanging open, as she carefully swept the path free of the small debris that I had been ignoring. She circled through the meditation garden. Behind her, the sand was swept clean, leaving the illusion of a perfect, changeless path.

"Do you like the new cleaner?" Saul asked. "Does she fulfill her Purpose?"

I jumped. I'd learned to ignore him *too* well.

"I didn't hire a new cleaner! We can't afford her." Reluctantly, I admitted, "She's doing a great job, though."

A happy cotton candy scent drifted to my nose. "We saw that the loss of the cleaning service might force you to act outside your Purpose. I am happy that she will prevent this. Our church elders will pay for her labor. "

"Wait—she was sent by the Teddy church?"

"Yes."

"Why would you...? What do you see as my Purpose?"

"Being a minister," Saul answered. His ear tufts swiveled forward. "Preaching."

Something clicked into place. "Are you the reason that five humans and one Teddy always attend my sermons? But never the same individuals twice?"

"Yes."

"Hmph." I stared at that perfect, unmarred path in front of me. "I swore I'd serve God, and there's a lot more to that than preaching or going to church, though many humans forget it."

Saul's ear tufts flicked back and forth. "Your Purpose is to be a preacher. One who preaches."

Preaching to a church that might as well be as empty and perfect as the sand in front of me, I thought.

"There are a few other things I should tend to." I rose and stalked across the path, kicking up sand with every step. I left my scribbled, incomplete sermon notes behind. Saul followed in my footsteps, trailed by a distressed odor of burnt toast.

When I walked through the door of Tamir's Café, I noticed the dread that had burdened me on my last visit was gone. The smells of ginger and garlic seemed more intense, the golden stone walls more solid, and the view of a bustling Moroccan marketplace more vivid.

There were other outlooks that the windows didn't show, things that I thought the prosperous people dining at Tamir's should be made aware of.

When the maître d' asked if I had a reservation, I told him that I was here to pick up a delivery for the Lowertown district. He didn't even bother to check his book. Nobody from Lowertown would ever be able to afford a meal at Tamir's, he informed me.

"We'll see about that." I strode into the dining room, sat beside a particularly well-dressed couple, and began to tell them some of the things that I'd seen in the poorest section of town.

A few anecdotes offered tableside, a solemn and sorrowful stare, and suddenly diners were volunteering their leftovers—or even their whole dinner, in a couple of cases. I think they must have had guilty consciences. Tamir himself quickly overruled his maître d' and magically came up with a "delivery" of not-quite-perfect food for Lowertown. I smiled, accepted it graciously, and left, trailed by my furry pink shadow.

After I set up a free food stand, it took a while for the poor folk to believe I was genuine, and they still tried to find the catch.

"Why are you doing this?" asked one man, a sand miner who'd lost his legs and his livelihood in the same sinkhole collapse. Either he was one of the unfortunates whose immune systems rejected factory flesh, or miners didn't have the same deluxe healthcare package that us military grunts did.

I set a bowl of lamb tagine in front of him. "God ordered those who believe in Him to feed the hungry."

"I don't see any other preachers out here."

"I'm not preaching, am I? You asked why I'm doing this. I'm here not as a preacher, but as a woman who takes her marching orders from God."

The unhappy burnt-toast smell strengthened. Saul didn't like me doing things he didn't consider preacher work. The sand miner didn't seem convinced either, but he took the food and rolled away in his primitive wheelchair. I watched him until his wheelchair slinky-stepped down the stairs to the transit tube and out of sight.

I felt more relaxed than I had in weeks. I didn't have to worry about whether I was succeeding or failing as a preacher, or about whether the Teddies were boxing me into a corner of my own making. All I had to do was feed the hungry.

A roiling stench of burnt rubber wiped the smile right off my face. I turned, intending to tell Saul that if my feeding the hungry bothered him that much, he should stick to following members of his own church.

Saul wasn't even looking at me. Another Teddy stood in the shadows, watching us. Unlike healthy, plump Teddies, this one's limbs were stick-thin and insectile. His skin hung in loose folds. His fur was thin and patchy.

"Come on," I called, gesturing encouragingly. He edged nearer.

"He should not be this close to us," Saul said.

"What's wrong with him? Is he sick?"

"He is starving." Saul turned away.

My mind raced. "If he's starving, we'd better start with something plain. Bread, maybe."

"You do not understand," Saul snapped. "His Purpose is to starve."

Anger rose in me so strong and so fast that I had to freeze to keep from striking out. As if he sensed it, the starving Teddy stopped approaching. I bowed my head and fought to master myself.

Once I trusted myself to speak, I said, "Right now my Purpose is to feed the hungry. Your job is to help me. He's hungry." My voice was flat and hard. I did not sound like myself. I handed Saul a piece of flatbread and a cup of mint tea. "Give him the food."

I gagged as Saul's burnt-rubber stench intensified. The humans scattered, leaving just me and the two Teddies. The starving Teddy edged closer. Saul stared at me.

"Go on." I confess I felt a certain harsh satisfaction at putting *him* into an uncomfortable position for a change.

"I can't! It is not right! It is against his Purpose."

"Choose."

"There should not *be* choice! There is only one way! Every creature has only one Purpose! Without that—without that, there can be no God!"

My satisfaction leaked away. He was struggling, as I had

struggled once. I placed my hand on his shoulder. "We have free will so that we can choose. Every action that we make, we choose. Making a choice once doesn't end that. Every day, you wake up and have to decide whether to continue abiding by that choice. And every day, each decision you make leads to another choice. Without choice—without the *difficulty* of choice—our actions would be valueless."

The starving Teddy stopped a foot away from our food stand. He waited passively, as if it had taken all his energy even to come this close to the forbidden food.

Saul trembled under my touch.

"You don't have to hand it to him," I said. "All you have to do is put it on the counter in front of him. Then you will have helped me."

Saul shook like a dying man, but he set the food on the counter and even nudged it closer to the starving Teddy. The Teddy seized the food and fled. I don't know if he ate it. I don't know where he went. My attention was all on Saul.

After a few minutes, Saul stopped shaking. The stench of burnt rubber dissipated, banished by a clean, green smell, like grass after the rain.

He didn't say another word until we were back at my church, sitting in the meditation garden.

"I have found my Purpose," he announced.

"What's that?"

"My Purpose is to study the philosophy of this 'free will' you believe in, this idea that we are always making choices and that this is good."

I let myself smile a little bit. "Well, you can change your mind at any time."

His response was deadly serious. "Not anymore."

My smile slipped and then came back stronger. "Not *yet*," I corrected.

I still struggle with writing sermons, and I still preach to a mostly empty church. Only a few new parishioners have returned. Saul gives my sermons only polite attention, but he follows in my footsteps everywhere I go, and I go everywhere.

* * *

This story first appeared in the After Dinner Conversation—December 2020 issue.

Discussion Questions

1. The Teddies believe that "God could only become real when we all became fully the thing that we were, when we achieved Purpose" and that those who cannot find their purpose are reincarnated until they are able to find it. What would be the cultural ramifications of this belief system?

2. Does the Teddies' faith have a place for the sins of Christianity: envy, pride, lust, etc.? How do you think the Teddies would explain the place of "sin" in their faith?

3. In a deeper sense, what do you think the Teddies mean by the word "Purpose?" Is there a faith/philosophy on Earth that best compares to their use of the word "Purpose?"

4. What do you think would happen in the Teddy culture if a person found a new Purpose or didn't like their Purpose? How is Purpose in the Teddy culture the same as, or different than, a caste system?

5. The narrator believes the Purpose of a preacher is to both preach and to help others. Is the difference between the narrator and Saul simply different definitions of the role of a preacher, or is it deeper than that?

6. The narrator tells Saul, "Without the *difficulty* of choice—our actions would be valueless." Do you agree with this statement? Can you think of a counterexample, where a choice is easy, but still has value?

* * *

The Devil You Know

David Wiseman

* * *

Content Disclosure: Mild Language

* * *

I met the Devil today. He was walking down Main Street, right by the undertaker in B____, which is a little town near here, and which, for obvious reasons, I'd better not name. I recognized him straightaway because he had furry legs with hooves for feet. Well, almost right away. At first, I thought he was just some guy in fancy dress, but who dresses up like that on Christmas Eve? Not only that, he clip-clopped as he walked, and who has an outfit with sound effects?

And he wasn't alone.

He had at least two smaller devils with him. I say at least because although I can picture them now, the edges of that picture are a little fuzzy, so yes, two for sure but maybe three. I took them for boys out with their dad doing last-minute shopping, looking for something for their mom, so two fits the picture I have in my mind. But who dresses their kids up in fancy dress to match their dad?

I was so taken by the dad's legs—well, all the way from his chest down, the more I think about it—and the clip-clopping, that even now his face is hard to place, but I'm pretty sure he was wearing a hat, and when I picture that, I reckon it was a white cowboy hat and with some horns on it too. Horns like cattle might have with black tips, although I seem to recall by convention, they're supposed to be goat's horns. Besides the horns, the hat had a black band round it but wouldn't you expect the whole hat to be black? Maybe that old black-hat-white-hat thing isn't true after all. Either way, horns on a cowboy hat didn't make a lot of sense, even for a fancy-dress costume.

But then I haven't been to a fancy-dress party for a very long time, so I'm no expert.

The three of them, or four maybe, were coming right at me, the low winter sun straight in their eyes. There's not space for four abreast outside the undertaker's so I stepped off the path into the road to make room. Maybe they hadn't seen me at all, 'cos they just walked on till they were level with me and I just stood there gawping.

"Hey, fella, what's up?" said the dad, stopping and turning toward me.

What's up? Only everything. Where to start? So I mumbled, "Nothing." But I couldn't leave it, could I? "I just er... I wondered if..."

"Ah, surprised, eh?" He looked up and down the empty street before asking, "You're not from around here, right?"

"No, we just moved to..." I waved vaguely in the direction of my new home, about thirty minutes down the road.

"Ah, okay. Well," he said, ready to move on, "merry

Christmas to you."

"Wait," I blurted out, louder than I meant. "Who are you?"

He turned back to me. "Here I'm Nick, Nick Baphomet, other places I got other names, but I think you already know me."

"I'm not sure, maybe I do. You live here in B____? I wouldn't have thought in this sleepy little..."

"No, not full-time, just here for the holidays."

"You celebrate this holiday? I mean..." I hesitated over saying the word for fear of tempting a thunderbolt to strike me down, but he'd said it to me, hadn't he? "You celebrate Christmas?"

I looked again at the blotchy white and gray fur that started sparsely across his chest under his tweed jacket, thickening as it ran down his body to muscular legs tipped with shiny black hooves.

"Of course!" he replied. "One of my great successes, don't you think?"

"Your great successes? But..."

"Oh yeah. Jesus, Mohamed, Abraham, all the other guys like that, all mine." He smiled and leaned toward me slightly, so a cloud of foul breath rolled over me. "To be honest, I'm still pretty smug about 'em all. Used to be that there were so many gods nobody knew who did what and who to pray to, then I got the idea of just one god. Counterintuitive, right? But then the argument's over whose god is the real god. So good, eh? Brought more misery into the world than anything before or since. Yep, proud of that."

My head was reeling. Was this guy just playing me for a fool?

"Am I dreaming this? Did I die without noticing?" I protested.

"Hey no, not so far as I can see, you look fine. But if you're feeling bad then you should..." He looked back at the funeral home then thought better of it. "Okay maybe not there, but across the road in the Salvation Army store, they'll let you sit in there a while."

"No, no, I'm fine. The people here, do they know you're here, staying for the holidays? Don't they...?"

Don't they what? Get up a bunch of vigilantes and throw him out of town? Call out a lynch mob? A lynch mob in B_ _ _ _ was even less likely than me standing on main street casually chatting with the Devil, which was what I was apparently doing.

"Folk round here know I like a bit of peace and quiet when I'm in town, and I try not to bother 'em. Mostly, if they see me coming, they cross the street to run that little errand they nearly forgot, making out they didn't see me. It's like that most places I go these days, people mind their own business and look the other way. I appreciate that."

"Where else do you go?" As I asked, I thought of Hell and added lamely, "Down... there?" and pointed a crooked finger to the ground.

"Whooo-hooo, down there," he said in a spooky voice, pointing with a shaky finger to mimic mine. "No! Down there's all closed up, has been for centuries. Got too crowded, and besides, there was *nothing down* there that couldn't be done right here."

"So where?"

"All over, a week here, another there. We've got offices worldwide, all the big cities and some fairly out-of-the-way places too. There's opportunities everywhere."

"Offices? You have offices?"

"Incorporating was probably the single best thing I ever did. Meant I could delegate so much. Mostly it runs itself nowadays, I can put my feet up and do little more than watch, sometimes for decades. When I look back, I can't imagine what it'd be like running things in the old way. It'd be ridiculous; I'd never keep up. Gives me the shudders to think of it; there'd be a kinda creeping sickly goodness everywhere with only me pushing back at it."

"Let me get this right," I said slowly. "You've turned into some kind of jet-set corporate executive and you don't want my soul in exchange for my heart's desire?"

"Where've you been, friend!" He threw back his head and snorted a kind of cross between a laugh and a whinny. "Do you have any idea how much a single soul is worth today? Even a hardly used one like yours?"

I shook my head dumbly.

"Less than the cost of a cellphone. And a very cheap one, too, not one of your fancy things. Nobody deals in singles anymore. Everything's wholesale, bought and sold in bundles of two million here, ten million there."

His hooves clopped on the sidewalk, seemingly impatient to be done with me.

"The hat," I said shakily, anything to keep him talking. "A cow? And horse's hooves? I thought goat, did I get that wrong too?"

"We never liked that goat motif, and it was never my idea, but it kinda stuck for a while. But horse, goat, cow, elephant, it doesn't matter really. We're not strong on any of them. People see what they want to see."

Behind him, there was an impatient skittering of small hooves. In my stupefied amazement, I'd quite forgotten his small companions until that moment.

He looked down at them and ushered them out from behind his legs. From each side of him, a small version of himself peered up at me. There may have been a third between his legs, but could be I'm just imagining that now.

"Yours?" My question was superfluous, but I asked it anyway.

"Hell, yes!" he announced proudly.

"How old?" I asked, just like he was a regular dad and his cow-horned horse-legged miniature clones were regular children.

"These guys?" He seemed startled by the question and stroked his chin while looking toward the sky. I noticed he had a wispy gingery mustache and a poor excuse for a beard, like he hadn't shaved for a week or so but nothing much had sprouted. But then, if he was taking a few days off for the holidays, why not? He interrupted my wandering thoughts with, "You know, I don't really remember, but they're sure growing fast these days. Maybe eight or nine hundred. I know there was some bloody crusade going on somewhere, but then again there've been quite a few of them over the years." To underline the humor he saw in this, he gave another snorting bray, which the little clones echoed with their own high-pitched whinny.

I stared at the clone peering around his right leg. He had black eyes set in a pale round face, reminding me of nothing so much as a currant bun ready for the oven.

"We should be getting along," the dad said in that polite

way that you do when you're getting bored with too long a conversation with a slight acquaintance.

"No, wait, you can't just walk away," I cried. "This is too..." I stopped. Too what? Too weird, too scary, too ridiculous? "Too important," I asserted, hoping flattery might delay him.

"Look, I have some things to pick up and these guys are getting restless. Do you want an autograph or something? I used to specialize in doing things for good folk like you. It's Christmas, so anything in particular you'd like? Oh, but no selfies, I don't do selfies."

"I just feel as though I should do something. Anything, but certainly something. What will people say? What will my wife say when I tell her? They'll think I'm crazy, but they'll think I should have done something. Made some kind of stand." It felt quite empowering to say that much and I was a little surprised at myself, asserting right over wrong like that, and with this guy of all guys.

"Oh, now I get it." He grinned. "You mean do something like challenge me to mortal combat, then, using some magical powers I guess, vanquish me and save the world. That kind of do something." He couldn't have been more scathing.

"Well no, obviously not, but don't you think I should at least try?"

As I spoke, I felt into the big right-hand pocket of my parka in case I had a forgotten hunting knife lurking in its depths. The best I could feel was the plastic cap from a long-lost ballpoint.

"Okay." He shrugged. "If you like, but let's get on with it. I thought we were getting along fine."

"We were," I reassured him. "I mean we are; it's been nice

to meet you and your... boys." They were staring up at me from their black-button eyes, their little black-hole mouths hanging open like I was a madman, the like of which they'd never seen before.

"So what are you gonna do, stab me with those knitting needles?"

The knitting needles! The whole purpose of this errand had been to get knitting needles for my wife. They were protruding from the little paper bag I held in my left hand. But how to get them out, how to use them with enough force in a single strike and still retain any element of surprise? I stood staring at him, shopping in one hand, pen cap in the other.

"Maybe not the needles today, eh?" he said slowly, as one might speak to a toddler holding a box of matches. "So what now? I don't think you've thought this through very well. A fight, here on the street, in front of the children? What kind of example would that be? How long before someone calls the cops? Then you'll babble on about saving the world and in no time flat you'll be spending Christmas with the guys in white coats while your favorite chair will be sitting empty by your fireside."

Put like that, it seemed anything I could do was futile. I let go of the pen cap in my pocket.

"No, unless you really have got magic powers—and I'm pretty sure you haven't—then it's probably best to stand down your red alert. Here, let's shake and we'll be going."

Mesmerized, I took my hand from my pocket and proffered it limply toward him. He took it in cold, clammy fingers. It was like shaking hands with a dead squid.

"Well," I said a little lamely, trying to retain some vestige of self-respect. "At least I didn't sell my soul, I can say that. I didn't do a deal with the…"

They'd moved a few clip-clops away from me, but he looked back. It was my turn to squint into the sun. "You didn't do a deal?" he called back. "Oh, Robert, I think you already did. I'm pretty sure we've got a file on you somewhere. There's a file on everybody somewhere."

* * *

This story first appeared in the After Dinner Conversation—July 2021 issue.

Discussion Questions

1. If you, like the narrator in the story, met the devil, what would you do? What (*if any*) questions might you ask?
2. Traditionally, the devil is responsible for great evil. If, when you meet the devil, he is just going about his day as in the story, do you have any duties to fight or confront him? That is to say, do you need to confront an evil person, even when they aren't actively doing evil?
3. What do you think would have happened if the narrator had tried to fight the devil? What would have happened if he had successfully killed the devil?
4. Do those who do evil have the right to moments of peace and quiet when they are left alone, or should they always be confronted?
5. Do you think you have an obligation to always fight evil, at every turn, even if you are only equipped with metaphorical knitting needles?

* * *

Two Left Arms

Erika Lutz

* * *

Content Disclosure: Mild Language; Graphic Violence, Depiction of Self-Harm

* * *

It is to be unable to breathe but never to suffocate. It is to be unable to eat but never to starve. It is to be unable to drink but never wither. It is to scream until the vocal cords are torn to shreds, leaving the anguish to reverberate through the cranium for eternity for the ears that never stop hearing, the eyes that never stop crying, and the body that will forever know pain. That is the fate of the damned.

The writhing body, unblinking eyes wide and bloodshot, rolled off the end of the wagon into the maw in the earth. Its arms snapped and contorted horrifically in a way that vaguely resembled a spider flipped on its back—if the spider laid on a stovetop and, burning, so desperately tried to right itself that its legs bent in every wrong direction. The fact that the body had two left arms, its damning sin, might even go unnoticed by an ignorant onlooker. The body clawed at its face with those two left arms, at its throat, tearing its own skin apart and bleeding but never, never bleeding out. The infinite stream of thick, hot blood was absorbed by the soil, turning the damned into a headwater for an underground river of liquid fire.

"Praise the merciful one, our creator!" Father Barnabas cried out. He held the Almighty's holy text in his left hand of flesh and blood, though his eyes didn't need to grace the worn pages—the words were more a part of him than the straw arm hanging limply on his right shoulder, with its burlap fingers poorly guised in a black leather glove.

"Praise the merciful Almighty, our creator!" the collected faithful repeated, as several among them flung shovelfuls of earth over the wretched form. It didn't even try to spit out the first dirt that filled its mouth and throat or try to rub away the soil that landed over its open eyes. No pain inflicted by a mortal human, flawed and weak as they were, could be perceived amid such divine punishment. The faithful standing around the grave knew that the dirt wouldn't stop the cries, only silence them, but the silence was still better. At least they wouldn't have to listen.

"Praise the infallible creator, our savior!" Father Barnabas declared.

"Praise the infallible creator, our savior!" the collected faithful echoed, as enough dirt accumulated to finally begin to weigh down the body's thrashing arms. Mercifully, it was quieter now. The faithful knew its muscles wouldn't stop spasming, it wouldn't stop fighting against its new fictile restraints, but at least they wouldn't have to watch.

"Praise the righteous savior, our Almighty!" Father

Barnabas called.

"Praise the righteous savior, our Almighty!" the faithful responded. The body was no longer visible, but the ground appeared as though it was being tilled from within. More dirt.

"Praise the just Almighty who cleanses His beautiful and sanctified earth, where every living thing is created perfect and pure and holy as He intended. The Almighty, in His omniscience and glory, in His perfection and supremacy, knows every one of His children must have one right arm and one left arm. This is what is holy and good," Father Barnabas said. "This abomination, defiling His perfect creation with her two left arms, is now condemned to suffer in her wickedness for eternity. Damnation! Damnation! Damnation! Praised be the Almighty on high! Praised be the one who damns the wicked and tortures the unholy! Praised be the one who creates all things perfect! Praise! Praise! Praise!"

The earth barely stirred. As rains fell and the soil became more compact, the ground would settle even more. When plant life took root in the soil irrigated by the blood of the damned, the beating of the bodies against their earthen prisons could be mistaken for a breeze rustling the stalks of grass.

Dinah looked at the mound of earth. The body's name used to be Grace. Now it didn't matter.

Father Barnabas was the first to head back to the holy town, followed by the men wheeling the now-empty wagon. Grace's family followed close behind them, crying tears of rage and guilt—*how, after fifteen years of singing the Almighty's praises, could she still have not done as she was asked?* Grace's weakness was almost as wicked as her two left arms.

The other members of the faithful turned their backs as

well. Everyone knew it was just and proper and right for the sinners and abominations to be damned, yet they still did not enjoy standing above the wretched bodies bleeding, screaming, dying for eternity. This was attributable to human weakness—mortals cannot appreciate such holy suffering like the Almighty.

Dinah turned to leave too, but she felt a hand on her shoulder. When her baby brother was really a baby, it would be a tug at the bottom of her robes while he chewed on one of his fingers through his floor-length sleeves. Now he was taller than she, though he still hadn't filled out his frame. He was the same little Abel, merely stretched like taffy. His eyes were wet.

"Be careful," Dinah said. "You mustn't shed tears for the damned."

Abel's throat was tight. "She tried," he said. "She told me she tried. She wanted people to know she tried."

Dinah shook her head. "You know what Father Barnabas says. The Almighty only gives two left arms to the ones He knows are strong enough to sever them and wear their straw arms with pride and reverence for the Almighty's kindness."

"She couldn't."

"That's blasphemous; you know that can't be true," Dinah said. "Let's go rest before you think something you might regret."

Abel wiped his eyes on his long sleeves, trying to make sure the tears never touched his cheek, as if the welling in his eyes wouldn't count as tears shed. "She had the bone saw in her hand. She was ready to do it, but as soon as she made the first cut and saw the blood... she... she could never do blood... she blacked out." He stared at the mound. It looked like there was a burrowing animal beneath the surface, but they both knew better. "She said she woke up surrounded by vomit and blood... she couldn't do it."

"The Almighty knew she was strong enough to try again."

"She thought He would forgive her for her attempt."

"I'm sure He still relished her attempt, but she still gave in to her sinful desire to go through life as an abomination. She still came of age and rolled up her sleeves before the congregation and affronted the faithful and disgraced Him with her two left arms."

"She was afraid, Dinah."

"This is a dangerous line of thought, Abel." A dangerous line of thought she risked herself several times. It was hard not to feel pity at these burials—watching people turned into pain incarnate. She wasn't naive enough to think the Almighty wasn't privy to her internal transgressions, but she was a pious young woman, and perhaps the Almighty begrudged her the pity of sinners in light of her other virtues. Abel, however, needed all the good grace he could get. "Please, let's go home." She tried to turn to lead him away from the mound.

"I'm afraid too." His lips were contorted as every muscle in his face and neck flexed to hold himself together. His jaw quavered. "I don't think I can do it."

Dinah stopped. She turned back to face him. With trembling hands, he rolled up his right sleeve to expose his left arm.

"I'm an abomination," Abel said, his voice cracking. "I'm an abomination and I'm weak and I'm scared."

As long as she could remember, she had only seen him with his inky floor-length sleeves like every child before they came of age. He had bathed in them, played in them, as was right and proper and modest. But she knew he only wanted to hold her right hand. She knew he kept the arm on the right side of his body straight and rigid by his side to hide the fact it bent the wrong way. She overheard their parents' lamentations and knew where they kept the bone saw for when he was ready. And he *would* be ready, their parents had assured each other. Every time a damned soul was buried—he would be ready, he *would* be ready, he had to be ready. Dinah didn't know why she believed that if she never acknowledged her brother's aberration, she could will it into not being true.

She opened her mouth to comfort him, but no words left her lips. Her throat tightened, and she was left standing slack-jawed. She couldn't bring herself to say what she was supposed to say, what she knew the Almighty wanted her to say: "*I know you're strong enough to do it.*" She imagined Abel taking the bone saw from where they both knew it was in their house—tucked away in the back of the basement closet. She imagined him being forced to watch as he buried the serrated blade in his own shoulder and tried to stay conscious—at least long enough to keep cutting.

The only thing she could manage to say through the stricture in her throat was: "You're perfect." It wasn't a transgression because, even though she hadn't said what she was supposed to say, she hadn't lied. She believed it with her whole heart. Abel was perfect. Abel was her proof that the Almighty made the world perfect because he was her world. She saw the Almighty's brilliance in her brother's eyes, saw the love in his heart, saw the compassion in his soul—the year he spent all summer hand-raising an orphaned songbird, and now it sang loudest on the tree by their house. She thought about how every time they went for a walk, he collected wildflowers along the way to bring home for their mother. She thought about the way he made yarn dolls for every child on their first day of school, with girls' dolls having uneven braids and the boys' having messily chopped hair that stood up like a hedgehog on their heads. Even when he got better at his little craft, he continued to make them that way. He always said they had more personality, and he was right—those little dolls always made them laugh.

When she thanked the Almighty for light, for purity, for wonder, for everything right in the universe, it was all about Abel.

"How is that possible?" Every word was encased in shaking breaths. He started to point to the mound but Dinah grabbed his hand.

"I know you, Abel. You are kind and devoted and you love harder and truer than anyone in the world!" She took his second left hand in both of hers. "You are the best of us."

"But..." Abel was stammering. He rubbed his eyes as he spoke through shaking breaths. "Almighty forgive me; I don't want to do it. I don't want to throw part of myself away, I don't want a straw arm, I want..." He squeezed her hand. "Oh, forgive me, forgive me, I want to be able to hug and make snow angels and feel..." His words were consumed by gulping breaths.

Dinah rubbed the knuckles of his second left hand with her thumb. This arm, veiled by his sleeves, had clutched her robes when he was scared, helped her up when she fell, embraced her. She knew this boy; she knew her brother. She couldn't believe that the Almighty didn't cherish her brother, His creation, the way she did. He was perfect. She knew he was perfect.

"I will talk to Father Barnabas. He will know what to do," she said, conviction pulling her shoulders back and her chin up. She had no doubt there was an answer to this. The Almighty in all His benevolence, in all His forgiveness and mercy, wouldn't ask Abel to sever a piece of his perfect self. He wasn't like Grace—he was nothing like the damned buried outside the city. He was different; this would be different. She pulled his sleeves back over his second left arm, the cuff falling back past his fingertips to sway like a shroud over the fresh grave. "Go home and rinse your face with some cold water."

"Shouldn't I come with you to speak with Father Barnabas?"

"No, I'm your big sister," Dinah said. "Let me work this out."

Abel measured himself against her. "Not big anymore." He tried to smile at his poor attempt at humor.

"Don't be clever! Big *always*." She gently scuffed him on the side of the head. "Don't think differently for a second!" She nodded reassuringly. "The Almighty as my witness, everything is going to be okay."

Dinah knew the Almighty was merciful, was benevolent, loved and cherished His perfect creation, so she didn't know why, as she walked through the town, she felt afraid. She felt drawn to the shadows like a stray cat; she wanted to avoid glances. She chastised herself. She had nothing to hide from the faithful children of the Almighty.

More troubling was the fact that the knot in her gut tightened and moved into her chest as she entered the vaulted cathedral and met Father Barnabas in his study. His smile was the same, everything was the same. He knew her; he knew

Abel—they would figure this out.

"What is leading you away from the Almighty's light?" Father Barnabas asked.

Dinah stammered. She realized she didn't know what she was going to say. Suddenly, the truth was thoroughly lodged in her throat, sharp like a corn kernel. She coughed awkwardly into the sleeve of her robe.

He put up a pale hand. "That is alright, the Almighty will compel you in time," he said. "Let me fix us some tea." He turned on a small faucet before going over to the stained-glass window, retrieving his kettle and filling it. "Please take a seat." Father Barnabas, using his left arm to fill the kettle while his right arm hung limply by his side, gestured with his head to the ornate, red velvet couch on the opposite side of his desk.

Dinah sat in silence as the father set down the full kettle, went to turn on the burner, and then returned for the kettle before putting it on the heat.

"Is it possible for the Almighty to make a mistake?" Dinah asked. It was like jumping into cold water before giving herself a chance to turn back.

He turned his attention from the kettle to face her, and his gaunt and hollow countenance looked more ghostly than it ever had before. "No." His voice was cold and definitive, struck with the gavel of absolute truth.

"Father Barnabas..." Dinah said. She pointed to the rising smoke behind him. He whipped his head back around so fast she thought his neck might snap. As he yanked his right arm off the burner, Dina jumped up and raced toward him to use her robe to smother the flame.

"Thank you, Dinah," Father Barnabas said.

Dinah felt the urge to scrunch up her nose at the smell of burnt leather. She could see inside where the glove had been eaten away, the straw inside the tips of the singed fingers blackened into threads of crumbling charcoal. It reminded her of a ravaged forest—something that used to be beautiful and alive but was now just the husk of what it was created to be.

Father Barnabas used his left hand to pull his mildly charred right arm out of Dinah's hands and returned his attention to the tea.

"Did it hurt?" Dinah asked cautiously.

Father Barnabas chuckled dryly. "I didn't feel it; don't worry." He handed a small cup of tea to her before taking his own. "I can open a window if the smoke is unpleasant."

"No," Dinah said. "I mean when you severed your real one?"

Father Barnabas's expression went dour again. It was no secret that the father had a straw arm, although the congregation collectively did him the service of pretending it was. Although Father Barnabas had done as the Almighty demanded, he would never have a right arm of flesh and blood as was natural, as the Almighty intended. Shame and loss were sewn into his right shoulder. Father Barnabas gritted his teeth. "This is my real arm! This is the one I want; the one the Almighty wants me to bear!"

"Please, Father," Dinah said. "I only seek your guidance."

Father Barnabas exhaled defeatedly. "My faith was tested," he confessed. "But I came out more devoted than before. I was honored to do it, honored that the Almighty believed me strong enough for such an act of devotion."

"Do you truly love your straw arm?"

"I wear it with reverence, knowing I am living the path of

light as the Almighty desires," Father Barnabas said. "I know I will be rewarded with eternal happiness for my deference and so I love it, yes, of course, I love it. What kind of questions are these?"

Dinah picked at the sleeve of her robe. "When you are rewarded and join hands with the Almighty, will you have a straw arm?"

"Of course not, I will be perfect."

"Will you have your second left arm back?"

Father Barnabas sat up with a start and almost spilled his tea. "Almighty's forgiveness no! I will have one left arm and one right arm—both of flesh and blood. Perfect as the Almighty always intended."

"Would that be *you*, then, who joins hands with the Almighty? With a right hand of flesh and blood you never knew in life, that never touched a loved one or turned a page of the holy text or..."

"Enough!" Father Barnabas put his tea down so he could point at her. "You affront the Almighty with your blasphemous questions."

"But what if there are people with two left arms who are *good*?"

"Then they will sever their abomination of the flesh, as the Almighty demands."

"But what if they don't deserve to suffer so?"

"If you believe this, then you have fallen out of the Almighty's light and will be damned alongside them. Thank the Almighty for your left hand and your right—one of each, perfectly mirrored and opposite as was His grand design—and cease this treacherous thinking. I won't tolerate any more of this vulgarity."

All Dinah could see was Grace's convulsing form being swallowed by the earth.

"She was afraid."

She promised Abel everything would be okay. She thought she had understood what benevolence was, what mercy was, but she didn't know anything.

"I'm afraid. I don't know what to do."

A distant scream made her insides crystallize but the air smolder. She was out of the couch and into the hall faster than she realized she had moved. She ran back through the halls into the vaulted nave. Stained glass and carvings of angels danced up the wall and across the ceilings, and blood ran down the altar.

Dinah ran toward her brother, who reached for her with his one left arm. She cradled him in her arms and tried to grip his right shoulder to stop the bleeding. Abel's blood ran hot and sticky over her hands and her robe. He was crying. She tried to dry his eyes, but she only painted his marble cheeks garnet.

"You said you would love me no matter what," he said, through choking sobs and gritted teeth. She couldn't tell if his eyes were rolling back in their sockets or if he was trying to look up—see something invisible through blinding pain. "He won't."

"This..." Dinah couldn't speak, only shake her head. Her whole body was trembling.

"Please help me," Abel said. He weakly pointed at a straw arm, soaking up his blood as if the effigy believed it could really replace what her brother had sacrificed. "You're the big sister, big always, big always..." He seemed to be flirting with the edges of consciousness. Dinah tried to thread the needle he'd handed her. Abel's blood ran down her arms; her hands shook violently.

"You can sew it, you fix pants, I've seen it: thread needle, up down, rabbit over the hill, sew it on, hop hop, burrow, hill, everything's okay, going to be okay." Abel was rambling now. Her hands were red, and now the needle and thread were too. It was hard to tell if her vision was blurring or if everything was just being painted crimson. She finally managed to thread the needle and grab the dripping straw arm with its stained burlap skin. Tears washed stripes of blood down her face every time her needle pierced her brother's skin. She wanted to tell him she loved him so much and he was being so brave, but she didn't want to cry harder, to shake harder, to hurt him more, so she bit her tongue. Did her teeth draw her own blood? She would never know.

Father Barnabas walked into the nave with his flesh arm outstretched and a grin across his face. "Praise the Almighty for this holy challenge and praise this child of the Almighty for walking the path of the light! Holy! Holy! Holy!" He cried out. His voice echoed in the cavernous chamber. "The Almighty, our infallible creator, will reward your obedience! Praise this beautiful and holy day! Without the shedding of blood, there is no mercy! Praise! Praise! Praise!"

He came over to help Abel up. "You act in the Almighty's name and live in the Almighty's image." He looked at Dinah on her knees at the altar, needle still in hand and Abel's severed arm beside her. "You must be so proud. What a joyous and holy day!"

The father started shepherding Abel away. Dinah dropped the needle and grabbed her brother's second left arm. The bleeding was beginning to slow but the flesh was still warm. It still felt like her brother's arm—it *was* her brother's arm. She clutched it close to her chest and stood up. She was no longer trembling.

"Are *you* proud, Father?"

Father Barnabas turned around to face her. Abel was slumped against him, barely able to support his own weight.

"Are you proud to praise the Almighty who asks a sister to bathe in her brother's blood? Are you proud to praise the Almighty who creates that which He will not love?"

"Silence!"

"No!" Dinah stood drenched at the headway of Abel's river of blood. "I would sooner welcome damnation than join hands with such evil! I refuse to worship at an altar of blood! I refuse to sing the praises of a tyrant!" She raised her brother's arm in a crimson hand. "I renounce this altar! I renounce the holy word! I renounce the Almighty's name!"

Perhaps the greatest tragedy of damnation is that no mortal can truly conceive of its severity until it's too late. How can a mere human understand divine pain? Eternity? Even the damned already buried still didn't know eternity. Not yet.

Dinah gasped for air that would never come. She wished for death that would never come. She buckled to the floor and screamed. She writhed in her brother's blood. She clawed at her face, clawed at her throat, but the fire of a thousand suns, the piercing of a thousand shards of glass didn't stop, wouldn't stop. There was blood in her eyes and mouth, but she didn't know which was her brother's anymore. It was just red, hot, flowing, gushing, everywhere. She was vaguely aware of being lifted into the wagon.

She could feel the dirt on her tongue and in the back of her throat.

"Praise the merciful one, our creator!"

She could feel the dirt pressed against her crying, unblinking eyes.

"Praise the infallible creator, our savior!"

Somehow, her screaming wasn't quieter when the earth swallowed her, but twice as loud in her own head, just for her to hear.

"Praise the righteous savior, our Almighty!"

She writhed against her earthen restraints. Her bones snapped but never shattered—breaking, breaking, breaking over and over again for eternity. Blood ran into the earth around her but never drained—bleeding, bleeding, bleeding for eternity. This is the fate of the damned.

And so, the Almighty, in all His omnipotence, delivered His divine sentence. In all His omniscience, He watched her suffer. And then, the Almighty, in all His benevolence, was satisfied.

* * *

This story first appeared in the After Dinner Conversation—August 2024 issue.

Discussion Questions

1. What is the chain of logic (*if any*) that leads Dinah to believe there is no God? What are the strengths and errors in her reasoning?

2. How is severing an arm different than any other religious ceremonial sacrifices or requirements? For example, how is it different than circumcision?

3. If God declared our sky to be green (*though the color didn't change*), would that now be our truth because God said it was so? Or, would God only refer to the sky as blue because God only speaks the truth? Does God create the truth or perfectly reflect it? What are the distinctions between the two?

4. If humans are forced to review and interpret goodness and God's intention, is there anything wrong with deferring to a more learned interpreter, like a religious leader? How do you know when to override the opinion of a religious leader?

5. If you lived in this society with a right and left arm, would you defend those with two left arms who refused to cut one off? Would you defend those with two left arms who wanted to cut one off in the name of God in a society that looked down upon the practice of cutting off left arms?

* * *

Author Information

The Angel In The Juniper

Sarah Johnson is a writer, homemaker, and college sophomore from Washington State. Love of history, philosophy, and the forest all trickle into her wordcraft, which also appears in *Cassandra Voices*, *Solum*, and the *Chinook Observer*. She dreams of being a professor of church history, and of writing the Great Austrian-But-Written-by-an-American Novel.

Grief

Steven Ross grew up in the greater Philadelphia region. He attended the University of Pittsburgh and obtained a bachelor's degree in computer science. Intense reading and role-playing games—pen and paper as well as virtual—sparked his interest in prose and love for writing. His preferred genres include speculative fiction, science fiction, and fantasy.

Pneumadectomy

Harris Coverley has short fiction published or forthcoming in *Curiosities*, *Caustic Frolic*, and the *J.J. Outré Review*. He is also a Rhysling-nominated poet, with verse in or accepted for *Star*Line*, *Scifaikuest*, *Better Than Starbucks*, *Abandoned Library Press*, *The Oddville Press*, and *New Reader Magazine*, amongst many others. He lives in Manchester, England.

The House of God

Shannon Frost Greenstein (she/her) resides in Philadelphia with her children and soulmate. She is the author of *These Are a Few of My Least Favorite Things*, a full-length book of poetry available from Really

Serious Literature, and *Pray for Us Sinners*, a short story collection with Alien Buddha Press. Shannon is a former PhD candidate in continental philosophy and a multi-time Pushcart Prize nominee. Her work has appeared in McSweeney's Internet Tendency, *Pithead Chapel*, *Bending Genres*, and elsewhere. *www.shannonfrostgreenstein.com*; X (Twitter) *@ShannonFrostGre*

The Sacrifice

Kelly Piner is a clinical psychologist who, in her free time, tends to feral cats and searches for Bigfoot in nearby forests. Her writing is inspired by Rod Serling's *Twilight Zone*. Most recently, Ms. Piner's story "Euthanasia" was chosen as *The Best of 2023* by *After Dinner Conversation*. Her short stories have appeared in *Litro Magazine*, *Scarlet Leaf Review*, *Dragon Soul Press*, *Last Girl's Club/Wicked News*, *Rebellion LIT*, *The Chamber Magazine*, *Drunken Pen Writing*, *Lit Shark*, *The Literary Hatchet*, *Weirdbook*, *Written Tales* and others. Her stories have also appeared in multiple anthologies. Facebook *@Kelly Piner*

God is Alive

Ville V. Kokko is a postgraduate student in philosophy at the University of Turku, Finland, as well as an aspiring writer of both fiction and nonfiction, with a number of articles and short stories published in both Finnish and English.

Sacrificing Mercy

Henry McFarland is an economist and part-time short story writer living in Virginia. He likes to use fiction to explore how people deal with changes in technology, particularly those that lead to ethical conflicts or challenge our idea of what is a human. He has published stories in the *StarShipSofa* podcast, *Andromeda Spaceways*, and *Every Day Fiction*.

In Their Image

Abra Staffin-Wiebe loves optimistic science fiction, cheerful horror, and dark fantasy. Dozens of her short stories have appeared in publications including *Reactor*, *F&SF*, *Escape Pod*, and *Odyssey Magazine*. Her novella, *The Unkindness of Ravens*, is an epic fantasy coming-of-age story about trickster gods and favors owed. *aswiebe.com*

The Devil You Know

David Wiseman is an Anglo-Canadian writer who has enjoyed some success with his stories on both sides of the Atlantic. His novels appear under his more formal DJ Wiseman name, while his short stories have been published in a variety of journals. David enjoys reading both fiction and nonfiction, photography, genealogy, and in better times, travel, especially train travel. Facebook *@DJ Wiseman*; *djwiseman.co.uk*

Two Left Arms

Erika Lutz graduated from the University of Pennsylvania in 2023 with a degree in biology and bioethics. This is her first publication; her current book project is also speculative in nature and explores ethical themes. Instagram *@erikalutzwriter*

Additional Titles

After Dinner Conversation - *Technology Ethics*

After Dinner Conversation - *Crimes & Punishments*

After Dinner Conversation - *Bioethics*

After Dinner Conversation - *Nature of Reality*

After Dinner Conversation - *Equality Ethics*

After Dinner Conversation - *Research Ethics*

After Dinner Conversation - *Government Ethics*

After Dinner Conversation - *Business Ethics*

After Dinner Conversation - *Examining the Past*

After Dinner Conversation - *Food Ethics*

After Dinner Conversation - *Sex & Sexuality Ethics*

After Dinner Conversation - *Interpersonal Ethics*

After Dinner Conversation - *Interpersonal Ethics*

After Dinner Conversation - *Philosophy of Religion*

Or subscribe to our monthly print/digital magazine.
www.afterdinnerconversation.com

Additional Information

Reviews

If you enjoyed reading these stories, please consider doing an online review. It's only a few seconds of your time, but it is very important in continuing the series. Good reviews mean higher rankings. Higher rankings mean more sales and a greater ability to release stories.

Print Books

https://www.afterdinnerconversation.com

Purchase our growing collection of print anthologies, "Best of," and themed print book collections. Available from our website, online bookstores, and by order from your local bookstore.

Podcast Discussions/Audiobooks

https://www.afterdinnerconversation.com/podcastlinks

Listen to our podcast discussions and audiobooks of After Dinner Conversation short stories on Apple, Spotify, or wherever podcasts are played. Or, if you prefer, watch the podcasts on our YouTube channel or download the .mp3 file directly from our website.

Patreon

https://www.patreon.com/afterdinnerconversation

Get early access to short stories and ad-free podcasts. New supporters also get a free digital copy of the anthology *After Dinner Conversation– Season One*. Support us on Patreon!

Book Clubs/Classrooms

https://www.afterdinnerconversation.com/book-club-downloads

After Dinner Conversation supports book clubs! Receive free short stories for your book club to read and discuss!

Social

Connect with us on Facebook, YouTube, Instagram, Bluesky, TikTok, Substack, Meetup.com, and X (Twitter).

www.ingramcontent.com/pod-product-compliance
Lightning Source LLC
Chambersburg PA
CBHW020022030726
47499CB00007B/2234